The Boy from Earth

To my children: Ed, Imo, Sam, Thea,
with thanks and love

Acknowledgments

Writing this book was an unusually intense experience. I've never stayed up later, or missed more meals. In addition to acknowledging the hard work of my publisher and editor, Kathy Lowinger, and copy editor, Sue Tate, I would like to apologize to my family for my inattentiveness.

Additional dialogue in chapter 14 is by John Keats. (I borrowed bits and pieces of his "Ode to a Nightingale.") That's just in case you thought I could write phrases like, "light-winged Dryad of the trees."

The scene with the carrot-wielding knights is based on an actual dinner-table episode. The rest of the story comes from the usual places in my mind.

1

Dream Landing

It's midnight, and I'm at a pay phone at a highway rest stop with a greasy receiver in my ear, smelling detergent from the bathroom next door and hot fat from the burger place down the hall, and waiting for my mom to stop dumping on me.

Have I done anything wrong? No. I'm bug-bit, dirty, and exhausted, but innocent. The camping trip was Mom's idea. The guy who left Victor and me on our own in the middle of the woods was her boyfriend. Ex-boyfriend, I should say. That's one good thing that happened. She dumped him like so much trash.

And now it's my turn. "Oh, Alan, Alan," she says. "Why didn't you phone earlier? Where are you? Do you know how worried I've been?"

My mom doesn't have to raise her voice to yell. I can always tell when she's upset. Some of her best yells come in a near whisper.

"Sorry," I say. In fact I *am* sorry – not for anything I've done, but because Mom is unhappy. "We're stopping for gas. Mrs. Grunewald says we should be back soon."

Mrs. Grunewald is Victor's mom. She's driving us home. She's the one who told me to call – even let me use her phone card.

I yawn. I hear a lone toilet flush in the bathroom next door. I hear the steady whine of the highway outside. I hear my mom sigh.

"Are you hungry?" she asks.

She sounds sincere, but this is a trick question. If I say yes, then she'll be upset that I'm not eating properly, and if I say no, then she'll be upset that I've lost my appetite and don't want her to feed me.

"Ahh-mmm," I say. I've used that answer before. Means nothing.

"It's all a nightmare!" She's back to being upset. "My life is a nightmare. You get back in the car, Alan Dingwall, and hurry home. I haven't finished with you!"

This is so unfair. Her life is a nightmare, so she's yelling at me. She used to yell at Dad when things were going wrong and she felt bad. Then he'd yell back. I'd hear them in my room, when I was trying to sleep. Now Dad's gone, and she needs someone to yell at.

I don't know what to do now, except apologize again. But I don't get a chance.

– Haven't you said enough, lady?

Oh, dear. That's Norbert's high squeaky voice. Usually I can feel a tingle in my nose before he speaks, but not this time. I guess my nose was too busy with the smells from the bathroom and burger place to notice.

"Shut up, Norbert!" I whisper, putting my hand over the telephone mouthpiece.

But of course he doesn't shut up. Norbert never does what I say.

– You go on and on and on. So many words. Did you eat a lot of alphabet soup when you were a kid? So your life is a nightmare, is it? Well, here's a news flash: talking to you is not a walk through the Paradise Gardens. Know what I'm saying?

I wince, listening to him. This is my mom he's talking to. And when you're thirteen – even thirteen and a half – you do not talk to your mom like this.

"Alan? Alan? What's going on?"

"I don't know," I say. Then I get an idea. Norbert has a high squeaky voice, so maybe she won't think it's me talking. "There's some homeless guy here at the rest stop. He doesn't know what he's saying."

"A man? A homeless man?"

"Oh, he's a long way from home, all right," I say.

– You're making his life hard, Mrs. Dingwall. He's the one living a nightmare, Mrs. Dingwall!

"He's using my name," says Mom, in my ear. "He's talking to me. How is that possible?"

I cast about for another idea. I don't get one. "Coincidence," I say.

3

"What?"

"Got to go, Mom."

"I'm not finished with you, yet!" She's actually yelling now.

– *But I'm finished with you. Good-bye!*

Oh, boy. Boy, oh boy. Silence.

– *Hang up, Dingwall,* Norbert whispers. *You've made your point.*

"Mom?" I ask.

She hangs up.

The food court area has picture windows. I can see Mrs. Grunewald and Victor standing under the lights by the minivan, waving at me to come on. I nod. On the way outside, I speak firmly to Norbert. I can't get rid of him because he's inside me, but I can tell him how I feel. "Don't do that again," I say. "It makes me mad!"

– *I don't blame you!* he says. *I'm mad, too. Mad at her! Talking to you like that. Doesn't she know how important you are?*

"Quiet," I say. "Here's Victor and his mom."

– *What am I, blind? I can see them perfectly. I must say, I like Mrs. Grunewald's baseball cap.*

"Just shut up."

Trucks whine past us. The moonlight makes them look silver.

"Did you get through to your mother, then?" asks Mrs. Grunewald, starting the engine. "She'll be that worried, if I know her."

4

I try to smile. "She's that worried," I say.

We drive down the highway, passing the silver trucks. I'm worried, and angry, and tired. So tired. I lie back against the seat. I yawn wide enough to swallow a gopher. The hum of tires on the road sounds like a song in a language I don't know. The moon is riding high on our right side. Nearly full, it looks like a Ritz cracker with a bite taken out.

What is Mom going to do to me? I wonder. And what'll I say back?

Mrs. Grunewald turns up the air-conditioning. When I feel the first blast of cool on my face, I sneeze three times in a row, so hard I have to catch my breath.

"Bless you!" calls Mrs. Grunewald, without turning around. "Bless you. Bless you." She seems a long way away, and each "Bless you" sounds fainter than the last, the words receding like ripples in a pond.

– *Thanks,* says Norbert. I want to tell him to be quiet, but I'm too tired.

The Ritz cracker moon is still there, in the same place on the window, but the window itself, like Mrs. Grunewald, seems a long way away. I reach out, but I can't touch it. I can't touch the seat in front of me, either. What is going on? I appear to be . . . no, I *am* . . . shrinking! I'm shrinking! A minute ago my seat belt was over my shoulder; then it was in front of my eyes; now it's over my head. I can feel myself getting smaller and smaller. The window is farther, and farther, and farther away. I'm shrinking into blackness, and the world is moving away from me, disappearing down a long tunnel.

I've never felt like this before sleeping. I fight to keep my eyes open. I hear Norbert's voice again, but not from inside me. He seems to be sitting beside me now.

– *Hey, Dingwall!* he says.

I close my eyes, a night swimmer sinking beneath the surface of consciousness. Funny thing, though. Even with my eyes closed I can still see the moon and the night sky, a poster on the inside of my eyelids. The tire noise becomes more insistent and high-pitched: the noise of a high-powered engine. Mrs. Grunewald's voice has faded to static. The sky begins to spin slowly and change color. It's a very complete and detailed dream vision:

We're going down. Our spaceship is spinning slowly, like a tired figure skater at the end of her routine. The surface of the planet below us appears for a second through the small curved window. I get a glimpse of rounded hills bumped together, with a deep valley cutting between them. Lightning crackles beneath a thick choking fog. Funnily enough, everything's the same color – lime Jell-O lava, mountains of emerald mist. It looks like this because the view screen of my space helmet is tinted green.

I hear Norbert's voice.

– *Hey, Dingwall!* he says again. I don't know where his voice is coming from. I want to tell him to shut up. I'm afraid Victor and his mom will hear him. I try to talk, but I can't. My brain doesn't seem to be attached to my mouth.

– *Hey, Dingwall, pull the lever beside you. Come on, move!*

I make a huge effort, and move my head. Now I can see where I am for the first time. And I realize that the dream is more complete, more detailed, and even weirder than I thought. I'm in a real working spaceship. There're instruments all around – gauges and dials and flashing lights. I can see metal brackets and coils of wire, and knobs and a single rounded window. I'm wearing a helmet, all right, and it's attached to a poufy suit. Like everything else, the suit looks green.

Sitting beside me, in a molded chair like mine, in a poufy space suit and helmet like mine, is a small figure – like a little kid, maybe three or four years old. As far as I can tell by feel, my helmet doesn't have antennae coming out of it, but his does. And his view screen is split down the middle, to make two individual screens. The kid is staring at a row of flashing lights.

It's like I'm inside a *Star Wars* movie, only instead of Han Solo or Anakin Skywalker, I have –

– *Be useful, Dingwall. Pull the lever!*

It's Norbert's voice, and it's coming from the figure in the space suit and helmet. He must be Norbert, but he's too big. Much much larger than the Norbert I know.

I still can't talk. But he can. He's bigger, but he sounds the same as ever.

– *Dingwall, I know your species is pathetically unfamiliar with space travel. But can you follow simple instructions? There's a brake lever over your head, attached to the bulkhead. The bulkhead is the wall. I can't reach the lever, but you can.*

7

Would you do it, please? Easy peasy. Slow us down so that the tractor beam can pick us up.

I feel my heart beating loud and fast. Everything is so strange. I'm not used to seeing Norbert.

I realize I've been holding my breath. I let it out, and take a quick gasp. Then a deeper gasp. That's better. I wonder *what* I'm breathing. It feels like air, but I don't know where it's coming from. Is my helmet connected to oxygen tanks? What happens when they run out?

It's a dream, I tell myself. Don't worry about it. You're not really here. You're really sleeping in a minivan. In a minute the dream will change, and you'll be hiding from monsters, or strolling downtown with no clothes on. Meanwhile, *enjoy* yourself. It's a dream. You're safe.

– *Pull the lever, fool!* shouts Norbert.

I open my mouth to protest, but the ground is rushing towards us at a great rate. The rounded hills look like folds of soft spongy tissue. There's a network of tiny dark rivers crisscrossing the folds. The lightning is continuous. I pull the lever. There's an instantaneous jerk, and the ship begins to slow. We now appear to be floating down. The lever must be attached to a parachute, or some kind of brake. Norbert checks his control panel, then spins around in his chair to stare out the window. He sighs.

"That was mean," I tell him.

– *What?*

"Calling me a fool. That was mean!" He's not usually quite so bad tempered. Rude, yes, but not mean. Not to me, anyway.

8

– *Sorry,* he says, without turning around.

Come to think of it, that's unlike him too. I can't remember him ever apologizing.

Something large and powerful grabs the spaceship. A huge hand is what it feels like, belonging to a monster. I can't help thinking of *Star Wars* again. The hand starts to spin us, and to pull us forward and down.

"What's going on now?" I ask.

Norbert is sitting very calmly in his chair. His hands are folded on his chest.

– *I've engaged the Underground Automatic Landing System,* he says. *The UALS tractor beam is guiding us down. You may feel a bit dizzy for a few minutes. The ship is rotating at a high speed to ensure an accurate entry into the landing tube.*

"Oh, good," I say faintly.

I know what he's talking about. Rifles shoot true because the bullet spins on its way through the barrel. I try not to think too hard about this. I concentrate on taking deep breaths. I do the same thing on the teacup ride at the amusement park – you know, those little circular cars that spin around and around. Toddlers love 'em, but I sure don't.

Fortunately, this ride doesn't last very long. A couple of gulps later, we stop spinning. In fact, we stop moving altogether. I begin to feel better at once.

– *Here we are,* says Norbert.

"Here? Where's that?" I ask.

He sniffs. Funny-looking little guy, with his arms on his chest. They're so short, he can just clasp his hands together. I didn't notice before. He doesn't seem to have any elbows, but I guess he doesn't need them. He wouldn't have to bend them to reach his mouth, like you and me.

– *Home,* he says, with a squeaky rasp as he clears his throat.

"Home? You mean . . . Jupiter?" Of course, that makes sense. Norbert is from Jupiter. He's always talking about the place.

He flicks a switch, and jumps down from his seat. A song is playing quietly on the ship's sound system. "Start living, that's the next thing on my list," sings a guy in a twangy baritone.

Norbert helps me out of my seat belt.

– *Jupiter.*

2

Champion-esque

Before we go much further, I should tell you a bit about Norbert. I first ran into him about a year ago, while I was cutting the grass. I thought he was a bumblebee. Turned out the bumblebee was a spaceship, and a tiny alien named Norbert – he introduced himself and everything – was going to be staying in my nose for a while. I had no idea I had an apartment in there, but apparently I do. There's a kitchen, hot and cold running water, parking, and everything. All I knew about was the running.

Norbert is from Jupiter. He's almost four years old – but it takes Jupiter almost eleven Earth years to go around the sun, so he's either middle-aged or just a kid. I can tell you, he doesn't act middle-aged. He plays soccer and drinks cocoa, and makes fun of people. He has a mouth on him, that boy. I don't know much about his home life, though he talks about his mom, and someone named Nerissa. She's a girlfriend, I think. He misses her.

Norbert and I have been through a lot together. He left me briefly to stay with k.d. lang, then came back to help me find my way through the wilds of Manhattan and the skyscraping forests of Northern Ontario. (That was the camping trip I just finished, with Mom's ex-boyfriend.) I can't tell you much else. I don't know how come Norbert has grown so much. I don't know what on earth – on jupiter, I guess – I'm supposed to be doing here. I think I'm about to find out.

The door of the spaceship is in the top. It unscrews. Getting out is like opening a pickle jar from the inside. We climb onto a platform that crunches underfoot.

We're in a big echoing cavern. Bright lights overhead, and a crowd in the distance. A brass band is playing a fanfare. I've been to the horse races a couple of times with my uncle, and they play this fanfare at the start of each race.

– *Oh, no,* says Norbert.

"What's wrong? Is that band here to welcome us?" I ask.

– *They follow my . . . the queen around,* he says.

Norbert doesn't sound very happy, but I am. A band and a queen!

"Great!" I say.

I've got a big smile on my face. I have no desire to go home. None. I never understood why Dorothy wants to get back to Kansas, when she's having so much fun in Oz. Why not stay and have adventures with your new friends? That's what I'd do. It's not even like Auntie Em cares that much about you – no way I'd go into the storm cellar while my little girl was wandering about in the middle of a cyclone.

Anyway, now that I'm not spinning I'm having a swell time. And why not? I'm on Jupiter, for crying out loud. How cool is that?

The trumpet call repeats two more times. I hear a rustling sound, like the tide coming in. The crowd is moving towards us.

I'd love to take off my helmet. I can't hear or move very well with it on, and everything looks green. But if there's one thing I know about Jupiter, it's that the air is poisonous.

The twin view screens on Norbert's helmet are flexible, like eyes. Right now they're crinkled at the corners, giving him a sad look. His antennae are drooping a bit too.

– *Let's get this over with,* he says.

I'm a bit nervous. The only royalty I know are Burger King and Dairy Queen. "What do I say to a real queen?" I ask him.

He laughs without humor. – *Don't worry. She'll do all the talking.*

There's a short ladder to the ground. We climb down, Norbert leading the way. The ladder is made of the same material as the platform. It crunches under my weight. I wonder what the stuff is – it's not quite plastic, but it's not quite metal either.

The steps are really close together. I use every other one, and then, to save time, I jump the last four or five steps.

The floor is spongy – it's like landing on a gym mat. I jump up and down a few times.

The crowd gets closer. I can hear individual voices. High voices, like Norbert's. I peer at the crowd. They sound like him, and look like him too. Little kids in poufy space suits with antennae coming out of their helmets. Kind of cute-looking, for aliens.

Except that they're not aliens. They live here. I'm the alien. I'd better call them jupiterlings. (Well, if I'm an earthling, what the heck else am I going to call them?) Actually, they look a whole lot like a set of astronaut action figures I played with when I was little. There was a space shuttle too, and a moon buggy, and an American flag. I sold the set at a garage sale, along with some *Simpsons'* toys, and spent my money on candy.

A single figure advances from the crowd towards us. She's Norbert's size, and has a white suit and round helmet-head, like him. She carries a bright stick in one hand, like a wand, and wears a blue cloak around her shoulders. A circle of fiery stones weaves around her antennae.

The queen.

Her voice is loud and clear, and it gets louder, and clearer, as she approaches.

"NOR-BERT! Is that you? Finally! What took you so long? Where have you been? I've been worrying and worrying. You don't call, you hardly ever answer your phone, I hear such stories, I worry myself into a standstill! And – oh, wait, I'm picking up a call, but don't go away, there's an IMPORTANT THING I want to say. . . ."

She drops her voice. "Hello? Oh, Cecile, you poor angel, how have you been? I was so mad when I heard. . . ."

The band plays a fanfare. Norbert sighs.

"What do you think the important thing is?" I ask, in a whisper.

– *There isn't one. She says that all the time, and then forgets what she's talking about. It's . . . the way she is.*

"Oh. Have you known the queen long?"

– *All my life.*

I puzzle over that one for a bit.

The queen has a phone headset wrapped around her head and attached to one of her antennae. She moves in a hopping, shuffling motion. She wears slippers, like Norbert's. More bright stones in them. The crowd follows. There must be a dozen of them here, huffling together like so many bunnies. They're not much bigger than bunnies, either. No one in the place comes up past my waist.

The queen hasn't stopped talking. ". . . and that's what I'd do, Cecile. Of course, I can get away with things because I'm the queen, so maybe you'd better let him keep his fingers. Listen, it's been wonderful, but . . ."

The queen keeps talking on the phone until she's right in front of Norbert and me. A bunch of small lights flash together like sparklers. I guess the jupiterlings are taking pictures of us.

"NOR-BERT!" She says his name as if she owns him. My mom says my name that way sometimes. "Welcome home! I see your mission to Earth was successful. This is so exciting to see a genuine earthling."

Without giving him a chance to speak, she goes on: "You heard what happened to Princess Nerissa? Of course you did. I remember, I called you. Terrible, just terrible. Stolen away while she was visiting here in Betunkaville. By now she's on her way to that horrible castle of his." She shakes her head. "I don't know what this planet is coming to. I don't know what to tell King Sheldon if he calls. Nerissa isn't due back in Sheldonburg until the day after tomorrow, but he could call at any time. She is his only daughter. Maybe I'll just say she's out shopping. Or hunting. Or –"

– *MOM! SHUT UP!*

It's a shout, almost a scream, and it comes from Norbert. I peer around, startled. I wonder where his mom is. He's staring at the queen. Her view screens close and open again, so that it looks like she's blinking.

And she shuts up.

3

Jupiter's Champion Comes from Earth

– Mom, I'm sorry, but you must stop talking for a moment. We don't have much time if we're going to save Nerissa.

She gasps. I suppose she's used to talking any time she wants – one of the many good things about being the queen.

The crowd gasps. I guess you don't talk to the queen that way.

And I gasp too. The queen is Norbert's mom. And, if his mom is queen, that makes him a prince, right? Prince Norbert.

Well, well. Prince Norbert. Didn't I say the queen said his name like she owned him? Didn't I say she sounded like my mom talking to me? Didn't I? I'm smarter than I think, sometimes.

The queen recovers first. "Oh, Norbert, dear," she says. "Am I babbling? I *am* sorry. It's just that I . . ." She catches herself, and covers her mouth guiltily. "Sorry," she says.

– *I brought Dingwall from Earth in a hurry, when I heard about Nerissa being taken. I do not want anything to happen to her. If Dingwall is going to find the Schloss in time, then we're going to start right now. There's no time for your kind of talking, Mom.* He sounds grim and determined, and a little bit nervous. In fact, he sounds like a kid chewing out his mom.

I don't pay too much attention to what he says. There's more to work out. Norbert has mentioned Nerissa before. Is she the princess we're after? I'd bet on it.

Poor guy. His mom is a queen, and his girl has been captured. No wonder he's acting strangely.

I have a sudden memory: Norbert telling me that the inside of my nose was a lot bigger than his place on Jupiter. What a liar. Imagine that. I had a prince living in my nose! And now I'm his guest.

Alan Dingwall, I say to myself, you are really having adventures.

Norbert introduces me to his mom, Queen Betunka of Betunkaville, calling me a champion. I bow, and call her Your Majesty. He introduces me to the queen's entourage. I wave. They clap. He joins them, speaking over the applause.

– *Dingwall comes from Earth to fulfill the ancient prophecy. Soon, we will not be afraid of the black day.*

Everyone shivers when he mentions the black day. The queen's space suit ripples, as if in a high wind. Her jewels sparkle. I wonder when the black day was. I can remember one day when I failed a math test, got punched by Mary

18

the bully, and spilled water all down the front of my pants in the bathroom, so that it looked like I wet myself. That was a pretty black day. There was leftover tuna and spinach casserole for dinner that night, too.

"Say, what is this ancient prophecy?" I ask Norbert. The whole cavern hears me, and they all start reciting. Listening to the high-pitched voices chanting together reminds me of the way we learned our times tables back in the second grade. Only instead of "two times two is four, three times two is six, four times two is eight," they're chanting about this black day. Turns out I have it wrong. It's *Dey*, not day (Norbert spells it for me later) – a *who*, not a *when*. This is what I hear:

> *The Black Dey preys on Jupiter.*
> *He makes it stupider and stupider*
> *By stealing our citizens*
> *From backyards, kitchens, halls, and dens,*
> *And holding them in durance vile*
> *In the Lost Schloss – his domicile.*
> *This castle – what a mystery!*
> *In plain sight, and yet none can see.*
> *Past bog and sudden mountainside*
> *It lies where nothing else can hide.*
> *The Black Dey's minions, great and small,*
> *Wreak havoc on our place of birth.*
> *Legend says his doom will fall*
> *When Jupiter's champion comes from Earth.*

The queen chants along with the rest. When the rhyme is over, she grabs my arm. "Everyone on Jupiter knows that," she says. "I learned it from our nursemaid when I was very young. I can't remember the maid, but I do remember the rhyme. Isn't that funny. Do you remember rhymes, Dingwall? Or maids?"

"My family has never had a maid," I say.

Norbert is casting quick glances around the cavern.

– *There's a lot to do before we go, Dingwall,* he says. *We have to see Mad Guy. I want to pack. And you'll need some slippers.*

"But you can't leave now," says the queen, her view screens open wide in dismay. "It wouldn't be right. You're back from an interplanetary expedition. You want to rest and do your laundry. Have you been wearing your bed socks? You know what the doctor said. And there's a dinner party tonight that I want you to attend. I'm going to ask Cecile and her daughter. You used to like little Natasha, do you remember? We'll have cocoa pancakes, I think, and . . . wait." Her head is cocked to one side. "Oh, dear, I'm getting a call. I'll be with you in a second, but I have a SUPER-IMPORTANT point to make, so don't go. Hello? Oh, Cecile, we were just talking about you. Isn't that wonderful. Listen, would you?"

The band plays a fanfare. Norbert's antennae droop like spaghetti. I know he wants to explode again. I know he wants to tell his mom that he really is in a hurry; that he doesn't like little Natasha, doesn't want to go to a dinner party, couldn't care less about bed socks. He wants to yell at her, but yelling is tiring. Anger is a steep hill. How often can you climb it? I know what I'd do if I was Norbert.

"D'you want to just . . . sneak away?" I whisper.

He nods eagerly and takes a step back. I put my finger to my lips and follow him.

The queen keeps talking. I can't help thinking that her name is not exactly a sound like gentle rain, or children's laughter. It reminds me of something heavy and wet hitting the bottom of the wastebasket. Be-*tun*-ka.

Norbert leads me around the back of the crowd. The queen takes another call. She's waving her wand up and down.

I feel real self-conscious, creeping around. Mostly because I'm the size of a killer whale. If I was Norbert's size, I wouldn't mind.

In about a minute,* we're at a swing door cut into the rock about halfway down the long wall of the cavern. Norbert pushes through first. I'm right on his heels.

We find ourselves in a quiet corridor – tall ceiling, smell of disinfectant. No windows. Norbert breathes a sigh of relief.

– *That's better,* he says. *Let's see if we can find Mad Guy's lab. I know it's around here somewhere.*

---

* I know time is different on Jupiter. So are weights and measures. But I plan to keep things simple. In this story, a minute's a minute. A day is a day (unless it's a *Dey* – but that's another problem). I may be inaccurate, but at least we'll both know what is going on.

He sets off at a huffling trot. I hurry to keep up.

– *Listen, Dingwall. About my mom. I should apologize. I don't know why, but she sometimes . . . makes me crazy.* He talks over his shoulder, embarrassed.

"That's okay," I say. "Mine, too."

– *Why would I care about a dinner party? Nerissa is a prisoner somewhere.*

"We'll find her," I say. "Don't worry."

– *Thanks, Dingwall. I really . . . really . . .*

He stops still and stands there. His hands are clenched into fists at his sides. His view screens are wide and staring. His antennae are vibrating like a tuning fork. Hard to know what to do when a friend is almost crying. I can't put my arm around him. I just can't. But I feel bad. I should do something. I decide to punch him in the shoulder.

He looks startled. Then he nods, and pokes me in the stomach.

So we're good.

That's when I hear the clitter-clatter of little claws. Much crisper sound than the huffling of the jupiterlings in their slippers. I peer down the corridor. Around the corner emerges a white lab rat. I know he's a lab rat because he's wearing a lab coat over a misbuttoned sweater vest, and thick glasses, which have been mended with tape.

– *Butterbean!* calls Norbert.

"I perceive you!" the lab rat calls back. "And I'm approaching your space-time nexus as fast as my organs and muscles and willpower allow. Welcome, my prince. I tracked your spacecraft on the UALS, and was on my way to the landing chamber to get you."

He arrives, panting, just as the speech ends. He runs on all fours, like a mouse, then climbs onto his hind legs to talk to us face-to-face. He's about Norbert's height.

"Hail, Prince!" he says.

– *Hey, Butterbean. How's Mad Guy? We were on our way to see him.*

"Welcome home, Prince Norbert. We're all extremely concerned about Princess Nerissa, of course. There's been no communication."

– *Yeah.*

Butterbean is staring at me. His eyes glitter like diamonds behind the spectacles.

"Is this really . . . him?" he asks.

– *This is Dingwall,* says Norbert.

"A genuine earthling. This is quite exhilarating. My blood pressure is rising rapidly. And so the despacer actually worked on him? He's awfully large right now."

– *Like a charm, Butterbean. Ordinarily, he's the size of a building.*

Butterbean's eyes widen behind the glasses.

Norbert introduces us. Butterbean is a scientist. He's responsible for something called the atomic despacer, which, apparently, is how I got here.

"Oh, please," says Butterbean, shaking his head. "It wasn't me. Mad Guy is the real genius. I just do what he tells me."

He holds out a neat, well-kept paw. I shake it without hesitation. A talking nerdy rodent is not the oddest thing that has happened to me today.

"If you choose to follow me to the laboratory, Mad Guy and I will be able to brief you both on the princess' disappearance and on our latest theories regarding the whereabouts of the Lost Schloss."

– *Excellent, Butterbean,* says Norbert, putting his hand on the little rat's shoulder. The royal touch. Butterbean turns to trot back the way he came. We follow his clicking claws.

4

Gifts of the Mad Guy

"This is the basement, right?" I ask.

Norbert nods. – *Betunkaville is a walled territory, with the royal palace as part of the wall. The secure strategy center, where we are now, is in the basement of the palace. You're in the safest part of the hemisphere right now.*

Butterbean is ahead of us. He stops to beckon us onward. "This way, my prince," he calls, in his light voice.

Norbert waves.

"Do you want me to call you Prince too?" I ask.

– *It would be appropriate. But I wouldn't expect it of an earthling.*

"Hey, don't knock us earthlings," I say. "We're saving your planet."

Butterbean reaches a narrow door, and ducks into it. Norbert follows easily, but I have to turn sideways to fit. My stomach scrapes against the side of the doorway.

The size of a building, indeed!

We're in an anteroom, rounded and dark. I feel like I'm inside a loaf of pumpernickel bread. Four guards stand in front of an arched doorway on the far side of the room. They wear uniform pants and jackets that stick to their skin like glue, and tight-fitting combat helmets. I recognize them at once – army men. I had a set like them when I was little. There's a guy about to throw a grenade and a guy with his rifle stuck out sideways and a pair in charge of a bazooka.

"Geez!" says the rifle guy, hoarsely. "Look at him!"

By "him," they mean me. They all stare.

"He's even bigger than they said," says one of the bazooka guys.

The rifle guy salutes as Norbert passes. He nods, and follows Butterbean into the next room. I follow at a slight distance. The guards stare as I crouch to get through the arched doorway.

It's a lab with benches and sinks and Bunsen burners like science class at school, only without Mr. Buchal and his elaborate sarcasm. (You want permission to go to the bathroom, Dingwall? *Permission?* Surely you jest! You have my enthusiastic approval, my unbridled support for your quest! By all means, go to the bathroom, Dingwall. I insist! And feel free to stay as long as you like!)

Mr. Buchal looked like a needle, and had a voice to match. The man at the far end of the lab is his exact opposite: short, round, and booming.

"Behold!" he cries, in a voice of thunder. He has hair the way Arnold Schwarzeneggar has muscles – lots, and all over the place.

"Mad Guy?" I whisper to Norbert.

– *Mad Guy,* he whispers back.

"Behold the boy from Earth!" Mad Guy declaims, more like a church minister than a scientist. He moves towards us in a weird rolling gait. An old old man down the street from me walks like that because he lost his leg in the war. I don't know which one (which war, I mean. It was his right leg). "This is a proud day for our planet!" he cries. "Welcome, Earthling! Welcome back, Prince Norbert."

He has his hands full, balancing a tray. On it are three thimbles and one good-sized cup. Steam rises from them. I can't smell anything through my helmet, but I can guess what's in the mugs.

– *Ah, cocoa!* cries Norbert. *Mad Guy, you think of everything!*

"Yes, cocoa! Cocoa for heroes!" cries the little round man, in his booming voice. "Cocoa and fruit. Come and eat and drink!"

He's smaller than Norbert and Butterbean – not even up to my waist – but he lifts the tray onto a workbench without spilling a drop. There's little cakey things as well. They don't look like fruit to me.

Trying to hop onto a stool, Mad Guy overbalances and falls to the floor. He then begins to topple slowly backward, arms flailing. His center of gravity is so low that he stops at an impossible angle, and then his whole body snaps back to vertical. His head, moving through a big arc, strikes me forcefully in the side of my right knee. I go down like a felled tree, bruising my shoulder under the space suit and knocking my head against the stone floor, sending my helmet flying.

I'm not seriously hurt. More embarrassed, really. Sitting up, rubbing my head, blinking in the lab's bright light, I realize two things.

First, that I can see. I mean, really see. When my friend Nick, who is extremely nearsighted, got his first pair of glasses back in kindergarten, his world changed for the better. He told me about it later. "I wasn't caring how much of a Poindexter I looked," he said. "I was like: Wow! That thing on the floor is my baby brother! I thought it was a dog all this time." That's how I feel with my helmet off. I can see. If you really need your glasses, you'll know what I mean.

The walls are smooth and kind of light brown, except for a dark square of TV screen. Butterbean's vest is yellow, and Mad Guy's wild stick-out hair is white, like Albert Einstein's. And Mad Guy is short and moves oddly because he's got no legs – just a rounded bottom half. He's like that Daffy Duck punching bag I had when I was little: I'd knock it down, and it'd come bouncing right back at me. Daffy could floor me then, and Mad Guy can floor me now.

The second thing I realize is, that without my helmet, I am breathing Jupiter air. And it's fine. In fact, it's beautiful – full of the heady scent of dark chocolate.

"How can I be breathing?" I ask Mad Guy. I'm not worried, but perhaps I should be. "Why am I breathing? I should be dead. Why aren't I dead?"

Mad Guy holds my helmet in one hand. His eyes are wide open and interested. His mouth has a humorous twist. "Who can answer that question?" he says. "Not me. I am only a scientist. I can tell you that you are breathing. I can tell you how you breathe. I can tell you that breathing keeps you alive. But I cannot answer why you are breathing."

He shakes his head, and pitches the helmet away. "You want a theologian," he says. "Or a philosopher. Or a psychologist."

"Actually," I say, "I want something to drink."

He laughs, and helps me up, pushing me back onto my feet. "Good for you, son. That's the right attitude. I am glad to see you. My name is Guillermo, but they call me Mad Guy."

I introduce myself, and lower myself slowly onto a stool. When I'm finally down there, my legs stick out the other side of the table. Butterbean is beside me. His whiskers are covered in cocoa.

"You have an exceedingly droll aspect, boy from Earth!" he exclaims. "Your outer integument appears to have been burnt."

I frown. "Are you talking about my red hair?" I've had it since I was born. I'm used to it. "It's that color naturally," I say.

Mad Guy is sitting up at the table himself now. He pushes the big mug towards me, and gestures to the plate of fruit. "Have some cocoa. And something to eat. You have a long journey ahead of you, and a difficult task when you get there."

He's talking about finding the castle and beating the Dey. "How long?" I say. "And how difficult?"

"Ah," he says. "Those are good questions."

I take a bite of fruit. It's flaky, like pie, and sweet. Weird, but tasty. I ask Norbert what it is, and he tells me it's pace, which means nothing to me, and then I remember him making a joke in school about the pace-trees of Jupiter.

"Hey!" I say. "This does taste like pastry!"

– *That's what I said. There's a huge pace-tree in Nerissa's garden in Sheldonburg. I remember we used to . . .* He stops, and his view screens go blank.

You've probably worked it out already, but I now realize that they're not view screens. They may look like they're part of a space helmet, but the two tear-shaped screens are his eyes. He brushes his arm across them.

– *Sorry,* he says.

Poor guy. Is this what love does to you? I wonder. Would I feel like that if the Black Dey took Miranda away? (She's a girl I kind of like, back home in Cobourg. Brown hair falling soft as summer rain, bright eyes, a strong right foot from all the soccer she plays.) I'd like to see him try to take Miranda. She'd kick a goal with him.

While I eat, Mad Guy asks me about the despacer Norbert used to get me here. Did it hurt? Could I feel it working? I tell him about being in the minivan and watching myself shrink lower and lower in the seat, until

30

I woke up in Norbert's spaceship. He shakes his head.

"The scale is so confusing," he says. "The idea that one of our spaceships could fit inside your nose is amazing to me, but not as amazing as the idea that you could then be shrunk so small that you could fit into that spaceship. And all because of the space between atomic particles."

I'd ask more about the despacer, but I'm sure I wouldn't understand. I mean, I couldn't even understand Mr. Buchal's explanation of the carbon cycle. I raise my cup, and nearly choke because the stuff inside is so good! It's sweet and thick and strong, like drinking a chocolate bar. I feel warmth and energy and sweetness flooding into me, like sunlight through a newly-opened window.

"This is wonderful cocoa," I say.

Mad Guy nods solemnly. "Yes, it is."

The overhead lights are out. An image flickers on the lab TV screen. Not a photograph – more like one of those artist's representations of the accused during a trial.

"Behold," says Mad Guy again, in his preacher voice.

It's hard to work out what I'm seeing. A vaguely human shape, billowy dark garments and a black helmet. One muscular arm clutches an enormous double-bladed sword. The image moves jerkily across the screen, like a cheap cartoon.

"This is the Black Dey, Dingwall: the enemy whose doom you are supposed to bring about. I'm sorry I can't give you a better sense of what he looks like," says Mad Guy.

"We interviewed hundreds of eyewitnesses in order to attempt a consensus," says Butterbean. "The discrepancies in their testimonies made this impossible. All they had were impressions: enormous size, a swirling cloak, a helmet, a long sword."

"The problem," says Mad Guy, "is that we got these witnesses after the Dey had finished with them."

"Oh. And I guess they weren't feeling well," I say.

"They weren't making sense. They'd been beaten by the Scourge."

I make a face. None of us says anything. None of us wants to think about what will happen to Nerissa if I don't save her.

"The Scourge?" I ask. "What's that?"

I hear a delicate slurping sound: Butterbean finishing his cocoa. The picture on the TV screen spreads a cold gray light around the room, like twilight in December.

"We don't know much about the Scourge," says Mad Guy. "We don't even know if it exists for sure. The witnesses are confused. One of them called the Scourge a spider; another said it was a crowd of people. The stories don't make any sense."

I lean towards Norbert. "Did you know about the Scourge?"

– *I'm just a prince, here. No one tells me anything.*

I peer closely at the pictures on the screen. I can't see anything to measure the Dey against. "How big is he?" I ask.

"Big!" cries Butterbean. "All the witnesses say that. And with a black helmet."

"Yes, but what does big mean? Big like a baseball stadium? Big like a telephone pole? Big like an extra helping of mashed potatoes?"

I can sense Mad Guy shrugging in the dark. "Who knows?" he says. "Big enough to be scary. Apparently you never see him and the Scourge together. We wonder if the Scourge might actually be the Dey, in some kind of disguise. Maybe when he takes his helmet off, he becomes the Scourge."

"One witness described the Scourge as a giant snake," says Butterbean, with a shiver of his own. Of course, he wouldn't like snakes much.

I tilt my cup all the way and find a trickle of cocoa at the bottom. Cold cocoa, but it's still really good. We watch the cartoon Dey swing his sword over his head, one-handed, and move brokenly across the screen. He looks like a medieval knight.

"Do I get a sword too?" I ask. "If I'm going to fight him, I'll want a weapon."

"You'll get all you need from the gym," says Butterbean. "I don't know about a sword, but there'll be something for you there. Slippers, for sure."

"Slippers?"

"For traveling. You'll have to cross a lot of country."

Butterbean clitter-clatters away to turn on the lights. I'm thinking about the slippers. How are they going to help my travel?

Mad Guy levers himself down from the table, rolls sideways, and bounces back upright again. This time I don't try to help him.

Norbert gets down too. – *Come on, Dingwall. We'd better be on our way. Thanks for the briefing, Mad Guy. The gym is two claps up, right, Butterbean?*

"Correct, my prince."

Mad Guy bows to Norbert, and shakes my hand. "Good luck, son," he says.

Butterbean shows us a circle in the floor at the back of the lab. About the size of a manhole cover, and bright bright green.

– *Clap twice, Dingwall,* says Norbert. *Then step inside. Like this.* He claps his hands once, twice. Then he steps forward into the green circle, and disappears.

I look a question at Mad Guy. "It's a transporter," he explains. "Clap once for each stage you wish to bypass. The gym is two claps up from here. When you're finished with the gym, come to the map room. Four more claps."

There's a faint hissing noise coming from the green circle. "It's really just a vacuum," says Butterbean.

"You mean it cleans carpets?" I joke.

"No," says Butterbean seriously.

I clap my hands twice, and step into the circle.

For a couple of heartbeats, nothing happens. Mad Guy frowns. "It must be the effects of the despacer on you," he says. "Your particles are closer together than normal, and the transporter is having to work harder. . . ."

He disappears. I lose my stomach, lose it again, and walk out into the gym, feeling lousy.

5

The Jim

It doesn't look like a gym, though. More like a messy attic or storeroom. My head reaches fairly close to the ceiling (I can hardly wait to get outside. I'm sick of crouching all the time.) so I get a bird's-eye view of it all. Even for a messy attic, this is a lot of mess. Piles of stuff in corners. Mounds of stuff on top of other mounds of stuff. Frozen waterfalls of stuff cascading from shelves onto the floor, covering it completely.

By stuff I mean, well, stuff. Different kinds of stuff. I don't know what any of it is, or does. It looks like you could wear some of the stuff, play with some, eat some, take some to school, and send some to your grandma. Some of it is pointy, like cactus needles or dentist drills. Some of it is soft, like bedding or pudding. Some of it appears to be moving. It's all covered in fine bluish dust. The dust hangs in the air, tickling my throat.

"Hello!" I call, and immediately have to cough.

I bet I'm in the wrong place. I don't see a door. The only way out is the transporter I came in by.

"Norbert?" I say quietly.

"Go away!"

Not Norbert, whose voice is shrill and vibrant. This is a dust-dry voice, wheezing, crackling, grumpy. It comes from a pile of stuff that might be a desk.

"Excuse me," I say.

Looking closer, I can see a pair of feelers poking out of one of the piles of stuff. They twitch, then there's a small explosion, scattering stuff and dust, and a small head pops out, attached to the feelers.

Two eyes climb up their stalks to glare at me.

"Can't you hear? I said go away! And don't take anything with you!"

"I'm looking for the gym," I say. I'm not worried – the creature with the bad temper is the size of my hand. It seems to be some sort of crustacean. A crusty one. I think I ate something like it one night at Red Lobster.

"So?" it says.

"Do you know where the gym is?"

"Yes."

Silence.

"Will you tell me?"

"No. Now, go away!"

36

I see something I recognize among all the stuff on the floor. I bend down. "Hey, how'd you get this?" I say, pulling it free with difficulty.

"A giant's bathrobe. Came in fourteen months ago. It's on file."

"It looks like mine." Made of black terry cloth, with a pair of pilot's wings stitched onto the bulging hip pocket. (My aunt works for an airline.) I wore it when I was the third wise man in our class Christmas play in grade 4. "In fact," I say, reaching into the pocket and finding a Kleenex package, "this *is* my old bathrobe."

I've always kept Kleenex in my pocket. Drives my mom crazy because she washes the robe, and the Kleenex explodes in the dryer. This is a fresh packet of Kleenex, and mine usually isn't, and this pocket isn't ripped down the side, and mine is, but it's my robe.

"Hey, and that's mine too! Wow!" I put down the robe and pick up a slipper. Corduroy, with a red tartan pattern and slippery soles. My favorite slippers ever. From a standing start, I could slide halfway across the living-room carpet in these.

"Yes," says the creature. "Flying slippers. They've been here for ages. They're on file too. Everything's on file."

"Flying slippers?" That's what I used to call them. It all comes back with a rush. Once I slid over the edge of the upstairs landing and flew – well, fell – down the steps to the front hall. I never managed the trick again, but I kept trying until I outgrew the slippers. My flying

slippers. "I think I'm supposed to take these," I say.

"*Take* them? Take them *away?*"

I hunt for the other one. I wonder if I can wear them. My feet have grown a lot since my sliding carpet days. Mind you, the slipper looks bigger than I remember.

"Put it down," says the creature sharply. With a speed I would not have suspected, it scrabbles out from beneath its blanket of stuff and scurries over to me, waving its pincer claws menacingly. It's some sort of crab, I guess. It moves sideways.

"Drop the slipper! Drop it now!"

"But Mad Guy said I would need it," I say. I find another slipper and pull it out. Yes, it matches.

"Drop them! Drop the slippers!"

You'd think I was a puppy.

This crab has two claws. The larger one holds a pencil. I hesitate, and lose. In a flash of silver lightning, the pencil jabs into my hand.

"Hey!" I cry out. "Careful, there."

"My name is Jim!" he cries. "I am The Jim – the only one. I am in charge here. And no one takes anything from me. They come here all the time, with their order forms and their requisitions, with their dollies and their carts. They try to take things, but I do not let them. 'This is a storeroom,' I tell them. 'If you take things away, it will not be a storeroom any longer. It will be a store.' They go away with long faces, and I laugh at them. Like this: ha-ha-ha. I control the room. I am the room! I am The Jim! Now," stabbing me again, "drop the slippers! Drop the robe! Never never *never* take anything from The Jim!"

I stand up. The Jim grabs onto a slipper with his free claw. I lift him too.

– *Oh, there you are, Dingwall.*

I turn around. Norbert is stepping out of the transporter circle, dragging two knapsacks behind him. – *I see you've met The Jim,* he says.

"Yes. I found flying slippers, but he doesn't want me to take them away." The little fellow is dangling from the slipper in my hand. He twists and contorts his body around, trying to stab me with the pencil in his larger claw.

– *Jim is in charge of the storeroom here.*

"He takes his responsibilities very seriously," I say.

"Put them down! Put them down! Put them down!" says Jim. "Put everything down!"

"Can you help, Norbert?" I say.

– *How? You look like you have everything under control.*

"Mad Guy wants to see us in the map room," I say.

– *Yes, he told me too. I'll meet you there, and then we can get going. Clap four times before getting into the transporter.*

"Hey, wait!" I say.

– *Oh, and bring this knapsack, will you, Dingwall? I'm a prince, not a porter. Yours is the big one.* He claps four times, steps backward into the circle on the floor, and vanishes.

Jim succeeds in wriggling himself into the slipper. He's now close enough to stab me with pencil again. "Drop it!" he says. Stab. Stab. Ouch.

39

This is ridiculous. I'm holding a pair of slippers with a crazy crustacean attached. I can't pull him off the slipper, but I wonder if I can distract him. I look around. I reach down to the floor and pick up the first shiny thing I can find. A silver tube – looks like toothpaste. "Hey, I can use this," I say loudly. "I think I'll take this . . . um . . . thing away with me."

"No! No!"

"I think I'll carry it away, and never bring it back," I say. "It's nice and squishy and fits in my hand." I hold the tube near the slippers and jiggle it, so the metal glints in the light. I feel like I'm fishing.

Jim takes the bait. "No-o-o!" he cries. He leaps from the slipper to the tube, and clamps one of his pincer claws around it.

"Drop it!" he says. "Drop it now."

The tube breaks, releasing a familiar odor. Not tooth-paste.

I don't make model airplanes myself, but I have an acquaintance who does. The fumes from the glue make you giggle and fall down and throw up, he says. I've never even got to the giggling stage, and I don't want to. I throw the tube, and Jim, into the far corner of the storeroom.

"Ha-ha-ha!" he cries in midair.

I move fast now, pulling off my space boots and putting on the red tartan slippers. They fit perfectly, as if they were custom-made Earth-size 9. How strange is that?

I shoulder the knapsack and clap four times. On an impulse, I grab my old bathrobe before stepping into the transport circle. I don't know why. There may be an association between the third wise man and the glue smell. ("Myrrh is mine, the bitter perfume.")

I hear Jim laughing like a fiend. Then I'm gone.

6

Map Room

"So, why do they call it the map room?" I ask.

"Why? Because of the maps!" exclaims Butterbean. "Haven't you noticed? Every wall is covered with them. This topographical map in front of us takes up the whole wall, and shows every feature of this part of the planet in . . . oh." He stops when he notices my smile. "You were making a joke."

Mad Guy and Norbert are both smiling too.

"Well, maybe a little one," I say.

It's a good-looking room, long and low, with smooth wood floors and hanging light fixtures that I am in danger of bumping into. The maps on the walls are the old-fashioned kind, with clouds puffing their cheeks in the corners, and dragons curled in the empty spaces.

Mad Guy is using a pointer on the big map marked TOPOGRAPHY OF JUPITER. "We've surveyed the whole hemisphere from Betunkaville to the sea, looking for the Lost Schloss," he says. "That includes the FRONTAL FOREST, here, the HIPPO CAMPGROUNDS, and this great area drained by the PARIETAL RIVER. We've flown over all the RANDOM LANDS. Nothing."

"What about the report from that fishing lodge a few years back?" says Butterbean, squinting at the big map through his glasses.

"You mean the guy who fell in the water? He was drunk. You can't trust those Parietal fishers, Butterbean. Not after sunset."

I'm wearing my slippers and bathrobe and knapsack. I spread my hands. "So where do I look for the Lost Schloss?"

Mad Guy steps away from the map. "When I found out that you were coming to fulfill the great prophecy, I went over the rhyme again. How does it describe the location of the Lost Schloss?"

I can't remember, but the other two can. They say the line together: *In plain sight, and yet none can see.*

"But that could mean anything," I say.

"What if the words *in plain sight* were literal, son?" Mad Guy says.

"You mean, it's on some plain?" I say. "Is there a plain on Jupiter?"

Mad Guy whacks the map with his pointer. There, on

the upper right corner,* is a great open area called PLAINS OF ICH.

Norbert stares up at me. I shrug.

Mad Guy points to the left-hand edge of the map, about in the middle. "Here's BETUNKAVILLE, where we are now. If you move towards the center of the map, you'll find something called BOGWAY FEN. See the frog on the lily pad? Good. On the other side of the FEN, you can pick up the PARIETAL RIVER as it snakes down through the RANDOM LANDS. Follow that river to the falls by the AMYG DALE here, and turn up. Now, what do you see?" He taps the pointer at a group of peaks that seem to be wreathed in fog. SUDDEN MOUNTAINS says the label. "Does that remind you of anything now?"

"Past bog and sudden mountainside," I say excitedly. The next line of the prophecy. Mad Guy beams all over his shaggy head, teetering down to the ground and then tottering up on his rounded bottom. He looks like a garden gnome.

---

* Upper right as you face the map, that is. I wish I could draw it for you. I love it when the story has a map in it. I never skip over maps, the way I do footnotes. Footnotes are hard to read, and usually have nothing to do with the story. *The peso, named for the Swedish philosopher Blaise Peso, is a measure of length approximately equal to a stride. A thousand pesos is a kilopeso, a unit of barometric pressure. For more information, see chapter 11: "Our Friends the Swedes."* That's a typical footnote. Since I can't draw a map, I'll have to explain the geography of Jupiter in words. Good luck.

Norbert is gazing dreamily at the bottom left corner of the map. SHELDONBURG.

– *That's Nerissa's hometown,* he sighs.

"I still don't see why we can't take your spaceship," I say. Norbert is zipping up his knapsack. Mad Guy and Butterbean are gone. We'll be leaving in a few minutes.

– *You don't know much about space travel, Dingwall. Sure, the ship would get there in a jiffy, and then what? There's no tractor beam to pull us down. Before we know it, we're over the next country.*

"You landed the spaceship in my nose!" I object. "You're saying you can't land it in the middle of a great plain?"

– *No offence, Dingwall, but your sense of scale is way off. You're used to the size of things on Earth. Here on Jupiter, everything is smaller. You wouldn't be here if it weren't for the despacer.*

"Are you saying my nose is big?"

Weird, I'm all, like, outraged. I wonder why. What's wrong with a big nose? Miranda has the greatest nose, high-bridged and narrow, like a knife blade, but she's sensitive about it. I told her once that I liked her nose, and she whacked me on the side of the head.

– *Big? I'm saying your nose is the size of a football field.*

Ridiculous.

– *And remember, Dingwall. The castle is hidden. It's called Lost Schloss for a reason. We have a better chance of finding it from close range.*

"You say there's food in these packs for a week. What if it takes us longer than a week?"

– *Then we're out of food. I'm not coming back until we're successful.* His eyes narrow, showing how determined he is.

It's a good line. I'm trying to think of something more classy than "Uh-huh," or "Sure," or "Me neither," when I hear the brass fanfare.

Norbert jumps in the air. – *Queen Betunka!*

"Your mom," I say.

The map room is at the end of a long hall. The double doors at the end of the hall open together. The fanfare sounds again.

Norbert pulls a string at the bottom of the big topographical map, which rolls into itself and disappears into the ceiling. Behind it is a window. First one I've seen on Jupiter. It has frosted glass, so I can't see what's on the other side. Whatever it is seems bright enough.

– *Come on, Dingwall. Let's get out of here.*

"Shouldn't we take a map?"

– *No time.* He struggles with the sash.

"But what about your mom?"

– *I can't stand her good-byes. She'll kiss me, and then she'll yell at me. Then she'll do them both together.* He shudders.

I know how he feels. My mom wears two faces too. Sometimes she loves me so much it hurts; other times . . . well, she doesn't.

The crowd noise starts to spill into the map room from the hall outside. I hear the queen's voice clearly.

"NOR-BERT! Where are you? I'm sending out invitations to the party tonight. Cecile's daughter is looking forward to seeing you again. Mad Guy, you said they were in the map room!"

Norbert succeeds in pulling up the sash. A gust of wind blows through the narrow opening and, with it, a gust of brightness. Norbert hoicks one leg over the windowsill.

– *Come on, Dingwall,* he whispers.

Is he really going to run away from his mom? I've never done that. Mind you, I've wanted to. I look back over my shoulder. The crowd is surging down the long hall.

Norbert leaps out the window, pulling me after him.

For a second, I'm blinded by the daylight. I have to squint to see. And what I see is a sheer cliff face flashing past me. I'm in midair, plummeting to my doom.

6A

Slippers

I look around for Norbert. Can't see him. The sun is directly overhead. Smaller than I'm used to – of course, it's farther away. I look down. I'm above a layer of cloud, so I can't see the jupiter. That sounds weird. The ground, I mean.

Want to know something? Falling is fun. This part is, anyway. I know that landing isn't going to be much fun, but, so far so good. I wonder if I can fly. I pump up and down with my arms. My bathrobe flaps and flutters. I don't slow down.

Still falling. The sheer cliff flashes past. My ears are popping like firecrackers. I twist myself around – harder than you think, with nothing to push off of. Oddly enough, I'm facing more cliff. I keep twisting around, and the cliff stays with me.

Wait a minute. If I'm surrounded by steep walls, I'm not falling off a mountain.

– *Dingwall! Dingwall!*

"Norbert!" He's above me. How did that happen, if he fell first?

– *Pull up!* he shouts. *Put on the brakes!*

"What do you mean, pull up? What brakes?"

It's darker. The sun has moved. I see a circle of blue sky when I look up. A circle? I begin to understand what has happened. Rock walls flash past all around me. I'm in a deep hole, like a well, and the sun has moved away from the lip. It's getting dark really fast.

– *We're in the Chasm!* Norbert shouts. *The Optic Chasm! We've got to get out. Put on your brakes, Dingwall!*

"What brakes?" I shout. "What are you talking about?"

He kicks his feet, and scoots down beside me. – *Your slippers, you idiot!* he shouts in my ear. *Use your slippers!*

"You're flying!" I shout back. "That's why I'm falling faster than you."

I stare down at my plaid-covered feet. I don't see an on-off switch, or a lever. I don't see how I can fly. "What do I do?" I shout.

– *Start by clenching your toes.*

"What? How?"

– *What kind of education system do you have on Earth, Dingwall? Don't they teach you anything useful? Imagine someone is tickling the soles of your feet, and –*

Ooh. I hate that. My feet curl instinctively, and –

Whoa!

The world stops with a thud. I feel a jolt in the pit of my stomach. Norbert disappears below me, shouting some insult.

I check out the rock wall. It isn't moving. I'm standing still in midair.

Wow!

Norbert flies back up to me, panting a bit. I check out his slippers. I can't see how he's making them work.

— *There you go!* he says. *Now, let's get out of here. We've already wasted enough time.*

"Could have been worse," I say. "We could have crashed."

— *No, we couldn't. Now, let's get out of here.*

He floats up past me, then turns to look over his shoulder. I'm staying still, afraid to unclench my toes.

— *Oh, yeah. You don't know what you're doing.*

He drops beside me, as confident and at home in the air as any seagull. — *Start by relaxing your toes, slowly.*

I try, slowly, and nothing happens. I relax my left foot a bit more, and immediately topple to the left. I start to somersault, so I clench my toes.

Now I'm stopped in the air again, but this time I'm upside down.

Norbert glides over.

— *Balance is tricky. It's important to do everything with both feet together,* he says quietly.

I nod. I can feel blood pooling at the top of my head.

— *Let's try it again. Relax your toes, and wiggle them. Remember to wiggle both feet together, or you'll spin in circles.*

Point the slippers in the direction you want to go. If you stop moving your toes, you'll slow down and then start falling. Clench your toes, and you'll stop. Okay?

"Okay." We nod to each other, but he's right side up and I'm upside down. Our heads nod in opposite directions.

– So begin. First try to turn right side up.

Slowly, I unclench one foot. The left one. Slowly, I begin to turn over. Blood rushes from my head. I feel better. I wait until I'm upright, and clench the foot again. There. Made it. I give Norbert the thumbs-up.

– Great. Very Sid, Dingwall. Now let's go.

I'm starting to get the hang of this. I smile at him, and put myself into the Superman flying position, hands forward. Not that Superman ever wore a bathrobe or plaid slippers. I relax both feet, wiggle all my toes, and fly straight as an arrow, backwards – into the wall behind me.

Suffering kryptonite, what a shock!

I hear Norbert's voice right beside my ear.

– Clench your toes, Dingwall. You're falling!

I am? Oh, yes, I am. I clench, and stop. "What happened?"

– What did I tell you, Dingwall? Point your slippers where you're going. Your slippers are not your fingers. In fact, they're at the other end of the body.

Thank you, Captain Sarcasm. I try to visualize the correct position for flying on Jupiter. "So, I should stay standing straight up?"

– Yes. Standing is good. When you're better at it, you can try somersaults.

He's joking, of course.

So I get myself upright, keep my feet pointed straight ahead, wiggle my toes hard . . . and fly like a bullet right into the wall across from me.

– *Clench! Clench!*

Oh, yeah. I'm falling again. I clench.

– *Boy, you stink. It's a good thing you fell into the Chasm. Way down here we're not going to be spotted by the Dey or his minions.*

"What are those minions, anyway?"

– *Minions are like myrmidons. Or helots.*

"Um. . . ."

– *Or slaves.*

"Oh, good. A word I know."

– *Slavery isn't good, Dingwall.*

"No. No, it's not."

– *Fly, now. You need lots of practice. And remember to clench to stop.*

Some time later – probably a short time but it feels like forever, like the last couple of minutes of a basketball game where they keep calling time-out – I begin to get the hang of it. I keep my knees bent for balance, and my slippers pointed where I'm going. I practise wiggling gently, every now and then, to keep airspeed. I can steer in a straight line, and make gentle turns.

I'm sweating from concentration. Remember learning to ride a two-wheeler? It's like that. It's fun, all right, but it takes a lot of effort at the beginning. I'm starting to get a headache.

Norbert is a horrible teacher. He makes snarky comments and keeps telling me to hurry. – *We haven't got all day, you blockhead!* he shouts.

"I'm doing the best I can!" I snap back. "You want to leave? Go ahead. Try to find the castle and rescue the princess by yourself. But I thought you needed me. If you want my help, then shut up, you . . . poopy prince!"

I'm so mad I fly right up to him, sheering off at the last minute. He twists his legs around somehow to back up. I haven't mastered that move yet. I point my slippers upwards. I'm sick of the dimness, down here in the Chasm. The circle of sky way up above looks blue and bright.

It takes Norbert a minute to catch me.

– *Hey, Dingwall, where are you going?*

I don't say anything.

– *You ready to move on, now? We've got a ways to go, if we're going to make it to Bogway Fen tonight. You know, I think you might be. Your flying looks pretty Sid. I had to push myself to catch up.*

"You think so?" On Jupiter, Sid means good. I turn with a smile. I'm ready to make friends again. "You really think so?"

Of course, when I turn, my slippers turn too and I fly right at him. He sidesteps in midair. I fly past him, clench to stop, and turn myself around with difficulty.

"Sorry," I say, awkwardly.

– *No problem.* He sounds a bit awkward too.

"Guess I'm not a real Sid flyer yet."

– *Sure you are. Not super-Sid, maybe, but you're getting there.*

"Thanks," I say.

We fly side by side for a while. The circle of sky overhead gets bigger.

"How deep is this Chasm?" I ask. "I fell so far. Was I just about to crash?"

– *It's bottomless,* says Norbert.

"What do you mean? This hole goes all the way to the center of the . . . planet?"

– *Farther than that. Mad Guy invented a photosonic probe, working on the intersection principle to find a target. When he tried it on the Optic Chasm, the readings came back as parallel lines. No intersection. No bottom to the hole. It goes down forever.*

I look back over my shoulder. The sheer rock walls of the hole go down and down, narrowing, darkening, disappearing. I shudder. Forever is a long way.

7

Minions

I want to stop for a rest when we finally get out of the Chasm, but Norbert says no. We've wasted too much time already, he says. He scoots away.

Everything looks bright after the dimness of the hole. The walls of Betunkaville are rose colored, with the sun above them. The land beneath me, covered in scrub bushes and stands of trees, slopes gently away from the declining sun. On Earth that'd be east, but I don't know where the sun sets on Jupiter. That's the way Norbert leads us.

Lightning flashes in the distance. We're too far away to hear the thunder. Norbert tells me not to worry; there's always electricity somewhere in the Jupiter sky.

I ask him to tell me more about the minions. If I'm going to defeat the Dey, I want to know about his servants. "I see them as little round smelly guys," I say.

He laughs. – *Those are* onions, *Dingwall.*

"Oh, yeah." They must be what I'm thinking of.

– *Minions are slaves of the Black Dey. Sometimes we call them hired hands because that's what some of them look like, but the Dey doesn't hire anybody. They're slaves, all right. They're not very big, but they work together, and they appear out of thin air.*

"Well," I say, peering around, "I can't see any hands here."

– *Just because you can't see them doesn't mean they're not here, Dingwall. Back on Earth, people couldn't see me.*

Norbert leads the way. I'm on his left, but behind. His slippers are perfectly still in the air. Mine keep sliding to one side, pushing me off course. I have to work harder than he does to keep up.

I wonder where everyone is. The countryside below us looks like Old Mother Hubbard's cupboard. I ask Norbert about it, and he tells a strange and disturbing story. – *This land wasn't always empty,* he says, poking his arms out. *It used to be prime pasture for rocking horses.*

"With saddles and big staring eyes and handles you can hang on to?" I say. I had one like that.

– *Many years ago, this land was filled with them. They were everywhere, rocking wild and free. Brown, red, purple, black, orange . . . all the colors of the ice-cream parlor. And the Black Dey came by and decided that he wanted to ride a rocking horse, so he caught one and climbed on, but he was too big, and he broke the rocking horse. He caught another one, and tried again, but he broke that horse too. He tried again, and again.*

56

The more horses he broke, the more he felt he just had to ride one. He caught them one by one, and sat on them, and broke their backs. And now they're gone.

Ew.

– That's the Dey's source of strength. Need. He doesn't want anything; he needs it. He has to have it. And he's stubborn and determined. He never learned that he was too big for the rocking horses. But he never stopped wanting to ride one. He caught every last horse in the land and sat on them and crushed them all to death.

I swallow. I don't feel well. I wonder what happened to my rocking horse.

We fly on. The empty land rolls beneath our slippers. The sun sinks behind us. I keep staring at the sky because it looks so strange with four moons in it. Norbert is on the lookout, checking the horizon, left to right, right to left. I'm feeling hungry, but I don't like to ask to stop.

– Look, Dingwall!

"What? Where?"

– Minions! says Norbert, pointing. *Behind those bushes. Now they've disappeared back into the air again. Did you see them?*

I peer over. "Nope," I say.

– Blind as a ball, he says.

I try to work that out.

We keep flying. The landscape changes. The bushes and trees become scarcer. Now there're grasses and mud, and more and more water. Bored, stagnant water. Some of it trickles gently; most of it just stands around. If the water were a teenager, it would be hanging around a street corner with its hands in its pockets. The smell is strong and swampy. The teenager had beans for lunch.

I'm getting tired. Correction. I was already tired. I'm tireder. I realize that my feet are asleep. I concentrate, trying to wiggle my toes. I forget to look where I'm going, and, "Help!" I cry.

Now my feet are pointing at a clump of trees, and, of course, so am I. I'm flying through leaves before I know it. I clench my toes, and stop just in time.

I'm hovering beside a smooth gray tree trunk. There's a branch in front of me, with a comfortable-looking notch next to the trunk. A perfect resting spot. I step out of the air and feel the springy give of the branch under me. After a bit of squirming, I'm sitting comfortably, with my back against the notch of the tree and my knapsack open on my knees.

That's better.

Norbert flies over.

"Can we stop a minute?" I say. I already have my knapsack open. "I don't know about you, but I'm going to see if there's anything to eat. I'm famished."

– *Good idea.* He hops onto the branch beside me. *Hi, Casey. How you doing?* he says.

"Who are you calling Casey?" I ask.

There's a Frisbee in my knapsack. And a TV remote. And a jar of brown liquid. And a packet of sandwiches. Mmm, sandwiches. I wonder what kind.

Rowf! Rowf!

At first I think it's a dog. Then I realize it's the tree that's making the noise. Of course a tree would bark. There's no wind, but the branches wave back and forth, like a tail.

Norbert leans over and pats the branch we're sitting on.

– *Good girl. Good Casey.*

"You're talking to the tree?"

Rowf, says the tree. I can feel it shiver.

Norbert uses that talking-to-a-dog voice. – *You're a good boy! Aren't you a good boy! Oh, yes, you are! Yes, you are!*

"But how do you know the tree's name?" I ask him.

– *There's a birch tree outside my window. Her name's Casey too. All birch trees are named Casey. Just like Casey here. Isn't that right, girl? Hey?*

Casey shivers a bit at the sound of its name.

I pat the trunk I'm leaning against, the way you'd pat a dog's head. "Wait a minute," I say. "Is Casey a boy or a girl?"

– *It's a tree, Dingwall. Didn't you pay attention in science class? It's a boy and a girl. Aren't you, Casey? Aren't you a good boy? Yes, you are! Aren't you a good girl? Yes, you are!*

The tree wags its branches again. Norbert pats it. I do it too, hesitantly, because I'm not used to strange trees.

We eat a snack sitting in Casey's branches. I worry about bothering the tree, sitting on it, dropping crumbs, but Norbert assures me that there's no problem.

– *Trees like to be useful,* he says.

So we sit on the branch and eat strange sandwiches. They taste like chocolate bars from a delicatessen. Pretty good, but, well, strange.

"What kind of sandwiches are these?" I ask.

– *Smoked chocolate.*

I take another bite. Okay, I guess. I take out the jar. "Can I drink this?"

– *Of course, you can. It's a liquid. You can't grate it or shred it. You can't read it or drive it. Your options are limited.*

I take off the lid, and pull back my face. "Yuck!" I say. "It smells awful."

– *But it works. Your feet will feel better immediately.*

"Huh?"

– *If you decide not to drink it, I might recommend rubbing it on your feet. They're working harder than usual today.*

Casey gives a whine. That's the only way to describe it. It's a bit like the creaking noise a tree makes in a windstorm.

Norbert sits up straight.

– *What, girl? What is it?*

The tree's long thin light greenish leaves turn over, showing their gray undersides.

– *Is something coming, Casey?*

ROWF!

– *Something bad?*

ROWF! ROWF!

Norbert closes his knapsack and motions me to do the same.

"Wow!" I say. "The tree understands."

It's like the dogs on TV that can add and answer the phone and spray the house with air freshener when they make a doggie mistake.

"Thanks, Norbert," I say. His hand's out to help. I let him take my sandwich container and the jar of brown liquid while I check the ground for intruders. I remember what he said about things being there, whether I saw them or not. Out of the corner of my eye, I can see his little hands fumbling with the top of my knapsack.

Casey is barking continuously.

– *Come on, Dingwall. Time to go.*

I freeze. The voice comes from behind me. I turn around. Norbert is facing away from me, wearing his knapsack, looking out through the foliage. One of his hands holds a smooth gray branch for support. The other hand is empty.

Then, what the . . . I turn back in time to see a pair of hands lift my sandwich container into the air. Not a person with hands – just the hands. Four fingers and a thumb, just like mine, only they're not attached to anything. They flutter around, like giant butterflies, clinging to the sandwich container, lifting it into . . . thin air. The container, and the hands, fade from my sight, like breath on a mirror. They're gone.

"Norbert, help!" I cry.

Meanwhile, another set of hands is finishing with my knapsack. They start to lift it up. I've been frozen all this time, but now I move, grabbing the bottom.

"Stop!" I cry. The hands do not stop. "Let go!" I cry. The hands do not let go. "Give that back!" I cry. Of course, the hands do nothing of the kind.

– *Get away from me, you minions!* cries Norbert.

The tree barks wildly.

I pull the knapsack away from the hands. I feel more hands plucking at my bathrobe, pinching, pulling, tugging. I flail around, sweeping them out of the way. There are so many of them. It's nasty, like being inside a swarm of insects. I shoulder the knapsack, batting away the hands as fast as I can, and point my slippers, ready to fly away.

– *Hey, Dingwall. Little help?*

It's Norbert's voice. I turn.

He's well off the tree branch, in midair, surrounded by hands – a whole cloud of them. He's being lifted higher and higher.

"Coming, Norbert!" I move towards him, batting the clutching hands out of the way. Norbert's covered all over like a cocoon, but his mouth is free. He's still talking.

– *I bet you guys think you're handsome! Really something – sorry, thumbthing! Get it: thumb-thing? Oh, why do I bother? I tell you what. You are the ugliest hands I have ever seen. I'm talking serious moisturizing problems here. Look at that hang-nail. Tsk tsk. And those cuticles. Haven't you guys ever heard of pumice or emery boards? Yes, you guys are quite a handful! Hey, Dingwall, I'm dying here!*

The minions work in silence. It's unnerving. I can hear the tree barking and the leaves rustling and Norbert talking and my own breathing. The thousand hands make no sound whatsoever.

I find a new technique by accident. Instead of grabbing the hands one at a time, I take them in pairs. When I do that, the fingers lock together and they grab on to each other instinctively. I set to work, pairing off as many hands as I can. Soon I'm close enough to get hold of Norbert. I try to pull him down towards where I am standing on the branch. The hands resist, pulling him upwards. I pull as hard as I can, a sharp clean jerk, and the hands give way all at once and Norbert drops into my arms. I lose my balance and fall.

We were close to the top of the birch tree. I fall halfway to the ground before I remember to clench my toes and stop in midair. The leaves and small branches slap and batter me, brushing off the remaining hands.

– *Good job, Dingwall. You've shaken them off. Now, go!*

I go. Norbert wriggles out of my arms and takes the lead, flying close to the ground. I follow. Some minions flutter after us, but they stay high in the air.

I take a deep breath. We're free.

The sun is setting behind us, but it's still bright out. We stay low, like swallows, skimming over the smelly bog.

"Can't we go higher?" I ask.

– *Let's see if we can lose the minions first,* he says.

I look up. The evening sky is a wonderful greeny purple color. Behind us I see a small dark cloud. It's going in our direction, following us, even though the wind is in our faces.

I have a question for Norbert. I wiggle my toes harder, to fly next to him.

"Back on Earth, you said that you would always be there when I needed help. But when I was being attacked by the minions just now, you couldn't help. In fact, I helped you."

– *Ah, that was on Earth.*

He says something else, but I miss it. A cool dank breeze hits me from the left side, lifting the back of my robe and making steering difficult. Norbert ends up over my head. I point my toes up to catch him again.

"What did you say?"

– *My job on Earth was to look after you, and prepare you for this.*

"For what?"

– *For what you're doing now. My mission on Earth was to find a champion. Once I'd found you, I wasn't going to let you get beaten up by bullies in your own school yard. I wasn't going to let you get lost in New York, or in the woods.*

I digest this for a moment. I was the best candidate. Huh? Imagine that. Another gust of wind hits from the side. This time I watch carefully and imitate Norbert, angling my slippers to ride the wind up.

He notices, and nods his approval. – *Well done, Dingwall.*

"Thanks. So let me get this straight. Your job on Earth was to help me?"

– *To help you, and to prepare you to be a champion. If you think back, you'll notice that every time you called for help, I came. And each time I came, you needed me less than the time before.*

I'm flabbergasted. Is that true? Maybe it is. After all, I'm enjoying myself flying around a strange planet. That would not have been true last year.

– *And now you're practically ready to be a champion, and we need your help. And here you are.*

Lightning flashes a little closer than usual. I jump.

"What do you mean, *practically* ready?"

I hear his exhalation like a sigh. – *The Dey is a real monster. Those pictures we saw in Mad Guy's lab don't show how evil he is. I wanted to prepare you a bit more. But then Nerissa got captured, and . . . well, I decided you were ready.*

"Oh."

My mind is whirling. What if I'm not ready? What if it's too soon? What if I need help? I don't ask these questions out loud because a champion doesn't whine.

"I see." Then I have to laugh at myself. Some champion.

– *There you go.*

8

Crime Dog

The sun has set, so I guess you could say that night has fallen. But it hasn't fallen very far. The quality of the light has changed, but it's not a whole lot dimmer than it was during the daytime because of all the moons. Four of them follow us, shining as big and bright as streetlights. If Earth were like this, there'd be no need for lightbulbs.

We lost the minions a while back. Seems our slippers can fly faster than the Dey's hands. I keep checking over my shoulder, but it's just to reassure myself. There's no cloud following us anymore.

Norbert drifts, almost bumping into me. He's tired. I'm tired, too. And I have to go to the bathroom. I hope we stop soon. I check my wrist. The hands on my watch are gone. The face on the dial opens its mouth wide to laugh at me. I look away.

– *There it is!* says Norbert. *Do you smell it?*

I smell swamp. Yuck. Then I get something different. "Smoke," I say.

– *That's Bogway Park Lodge. We'll spend the night here.*

Norbert skims off to the right. A few minutes later we reach a long low wooden building, with a smoking chimney and a porch all down one side. We land on the porch side, in the middle of a large square marked off in white chalk lines.

I look up. The sky's clear. "No minions," I say to Norbert.

– *They don't like the mud much. That's why we stayed so low. They like to keep themselves clean. As long as we're down here in Bogway Fen, we should be safe. We can sleep soundly tonight.*

I don't see a soul, though I can hear the whine of insects. "It seems an odd place to put a hotel," I say.

– *Well, Bogway Park Lodge doesn't do a whole lot of business.*

The building isn't much taller than I am, standing up. It's built into the swamp, so that the porch is on ground level, with steps going down from there. Norbert pushes his way in through swinging doors that might have come from a saloon in the Old West.

I follow, and the first thing I see is a big neon sign, blinking on and off. BATHROOM, it says. I head straight for it. Two minutes later I'm at the front desk, with ringing ears and a fixed determination never to go swimming again.

"ID required."

The desk clerk is a frog in a baseball cap and glasses with sequins, like your great-aunt wears. She stares up at me, goggle-eyed, past the burning end of a cigarette stuck in the corner of her wide lipless mouth.

"No one comes in without ID," she says, drawing on her cigarette until the end is bright red.

"I'm with, uh, Norbert." I'm still shaken from my experience in the bathroom. "He was just here – a little guy with a white space suit and big eyes. We came in together."

"Prince Norbert is known here," says the frog lady, softening momentarily. I should stop calling her the frog lady. The name plate on the desk says WILMA. "He didn't mention you when he checked in."

"Well, I'm with him. And I'm . . . important. I'm a champion," I say.

"You're still a stranger," says Wilma. "So give me some ID." She holds out a green long-fingered hand covered in rings.

On the wall behind the desk are four clocks telling different times, and four calendars with different dates. The months have funny names: Barch, Tamuz, Hekatombion. Somewhere on Jupiter today, it's Barch 15th. The ides of Barch.

"Well?" she says. "Don't you have a piece of ID? Something with your name on it?"

She takes a last draw on her cigarette, and then it's gone. Her tongue flashes out like a whip. Next thing I know the cigarette stub is smoking in the ashtray on the desk and her mouth is empty.

I jump back, startled. My hand goes to the pocket of my bathrobe, and I pull out a memory. A major-league baseball card. Just holding it in my hand brings me back to the summer when they came free inside cereal boxes. I must have had the bathrobe then.

Wilma stares at the card in my hand as if it were a million dollar bill. "Is *that* yours?" she asks.

"This card? Yes, it's mine."

Her mouth drops open and her tongue rolls out. "You're Fred McGriff!" she croaks.

I guess she thinks this card is some kind of ID. A driver's license, or something. "Me?" I look down at it. Fred stares up at me, calm and tough, bat cocked over his left shoulder. Number 27 for the Atlanta Braves.

"That's amazing. Let's see." She leans over the counter. "It has your signature and everything. Fred McGriff. You were right: you really are a champion! Imagine – Fred McGriff at my hotel. Wait'll I tell Wes and Steve. I know all about you. They call you Crime Dog, don't they? I remember when the Yankees traded you to Toronto back in the 80s. Then you went to San Diego and Atlanta and Tampa Bay. Why'd you change your mind about Chicago?"

I tell the truth. "I really have no idea," I say.

"What a career! How many years did you hit 30 dingers – seven in a row? And for five different teams! I always liked your OBP stats too."

Wilma knows way more about baseball than I do. "Do me a favor," she says. "Make a face like your picture there. Hold your hands up like you're batting. I want to see."

I hesitate.

"Go on," she says.

So I put up my hands, and glare like McGriff the Crime Dog. I'm tingling all over, as if my skin is magnetized. It's a memory flash. You see, I used to pose just like this in the bathroom mirror, with a toothbrush for a bat and a V-necked pajama shirt that looked sort of like a baseball uniform top.

She stares at the card, and then up at me. "I guess there's a bit of a resemblance," she says. "No one looks like their ID photos anyway."

For the record, I'm a whole lot younger, shorter, paler, and less cool than Fred McGriff. But there it is. I put the card back in my pocket. You know, it is signed. And it's in perfect shape. Looks as if it just got out of the cereal box. Weird.

Wilma checks me in, hops down from her chair, and shows me to the room. The skin on her back is bright lime green with delicate dark spots. "What are you staring at?" she says, turning suddenly.

"Sorry." I blush. "I've never seen a frog as big as you before." She comes up to my waist. Her legs are probably as long as mine.

"And you like 'em big, don't you?" She takes off her glasses and smiles at me. "Why, Fred, you devil!"

Her eyes bulge like grapefruits. Her belly hangs down. She flicks her tongue in my direction. It almost hits me.

"I better go now," I say, swallowing rapidly, hand on the door.

"See you later." She hops down the hall.

It's a bedroom the way the bathroom in the lobby is a bathroom. (Let me tell you about that, by the way. Pushing through the door under the sign, I entered a round white porcelain room filled with water. The world's biggest toilet bowl. The door shut and locked automatically behind me, for privacy I guess, but the exit door was on the other side of the room. In order to get out, I had to swing across the bowl on a pull chain suspended from the ceiling. My weight on the chain flushed the room, with a noise like a world championship milkshake-drinking competition. My ears are finally returning to normal now.)

Anyway, our bedroom is designed by the same person. It's wall-to-wall mattress. And soft! Stepping over the threshold is like stepping into a pudding.

Norbert hangs up the phone in disgust. – *No room service,* he says.

I can understand that. There's nowhere to put a tray of food.

I walk across the bed to the window, sinking into the mattress with each step. The window is just above ground level. Our room looks out on the chalk-lined square we landed on. Of course I now know it's a diamond, not a square. A baseball diamond. Fred McGriff. I shake my head at that.

One of the moons – the biggest one, faintly blue-colored – rides low in the sky, shining right at me. "Which moon is that?" I ask.

He's yawning. – *Sid,* he says. *You can always tell Sid because there's a smile across the bottom half.*

I look. I can't see the smile. I can't see the man in the moon back on Earth either. I shut the curtain, and let myself fall back onto the expanse of mattress. I sink right in, without bouncing at all. The mattress wraps itself around me like a soft and comforting hug. I don't need a blanket or pillow.

"Is it bedtime?" I ask. "My watch is broken."

– *Are you tired?*

"Oh, yes."

– *Then it's bedtime.*

I know I should wash my face and hands and brush my teeth, but I can't summon the energy. I can't even be bothered to take off my backpack.

"Night, Norbert."

– *Night. Oh, uh, Dingwall?*

"Mmm?"

– *You did well today. Learning to fly and all. And getting us away from the minions.*

I smile. I can't remember Norbert complimenting me before. "Well, they are my slippers," I say. I slide my feet out of them now. I don't want to be flying by accident in my sleep. Ahh, that feels nice. It's a relief to wriggle my toes and not have to worry about where I'm heading.

"Where are we?" I ask, with my eyes closed.

– *Remember the map? This is Bogway Fen, near the edge of the right hemisphere. Tomorrow we'll pick up the Parietal River, which will lead us through the Random Lands.*

"Do we have far to go?"

– *Are you anxious?*

"No, not really."

— Good. If you were anxious, it'd be far away. Everything seems far away when you're anxious. If we keep the rising sun in our eyes, the river under us, and Sid on our right hand, we should get to the Amyg Dale tomorrow. The Sudden Mountains aren't too far from there.

"Oh," I say.

— Mind you, I'm anxious. So my estimate may be wrong.

For a moment, all is quiet. I'm drifting away, imagining the Dey as a little guy with a bowling shirt. I knock him down in front of his castle, and ring the doorbell. Its chimes sound like a ringing telephone.

I come back to the hotel room. The phone is ringing. I ignore it. It rings again. Norbert picks it up. I'm feeling comfortable and warm, not quite awake and not quite asleep. A nice place to be.

— What are you talking about? A party? I don't want to go to a party. . . . I don't care how much trouble you went to. I'm asleep. . . . What do you mean, it's not for me? I'm Norbert, of course it's for me. . . . Who's it for then? . . . Look here, Melon-for-brains! You've got the wrong room! There's no one named Crime Dog here.

I sit up. Norbert is sputtering into the phone.

— Yes, I called you Melon-for-brains! Want another nick-name?

I cough to attract his attention. "Uh, Norbert, they mean me. I'm Crime Dog."

— What are you talking about, Dingwall?

"Not Dingwall," I say. "My name is McGriff."

— Hang on, says Norbert into the phone.

73

9

Barbie

Turns out that they're throwing a party for me – well, for Crime Dog – in the lobby of the lodge. The whole of Bogway Fen is baseball crazy, and it's not often they get a big leaguer in the neighborhood.

– *But you're not a big leaguer,* says Norbert.

"They think I am." I decide to wear the bathrobe, but leave the knapsack in the room. "You're coming too, aren't you?" I ask, at the door.

– *Are you kidding? I wouldn't miss it for anything. I want to hear all your baseball stories. Say, why do they call them bases anyway?*

"I don't know."

– *And why a shortstop? Why short? Is there a long stop?*

"I don't know."

– Okay, then, what about you? What position do you play?

"I don't know. First base, I think."

He snorts. *– Quite the well of knowledge, aren't you, Ding-Dog.*

"Crime Dog. My nickname is Crime Dog. Geez, do you think they'll want to know stuff like that?" I check the card in my pocket. "I play first base, bat left, and throw left."

– Come to think of it, Ding-Dog might be a good nickname for you.

"Shut up."

– Sounds like a doorbell with a cold. Ding-Dog. Ding-Dog. Heu-heu-heu. He keeps chuckling all the way to the lobby.

The WELCOME FRED MCGRIFF! banner stretches right across the room. The noise level is high, and getting higher. The frog ladies and gentlemen and children are croaking at once. They all want to shake my hand and get my autograph. Then they want to feed me. I say thank you, and take bite after bite, sip after sip. Soon I'm full of Jupiter grapes, Jupiter artichokes, and Eye of Jupiter, which looks like fried eggs but tastes way better.

My favorite thing is an almond cake, maybe because it's served by an apparition – an incredibly beautiful girl. She looks like a model. What is she doing here? She stands out among the frogs like a unicorn in a pack of gophers. Everything about her is long: she's got long blonde hair spilling out from under her ball cap, long eyelashes, and long long tanned legs. I quickly look away.

"Hi, there!" she says brightly, coming right up to me, holding out a golden square in her long tapered fingers. Her voice is clear and bright.

I stare at her eyes. Blue as cornflowers. I don't dare stare for long anywhere else. Like the rest of the crowd, she's naked. In a magazine, she'd be modeling perfume, or suntans. Or else she'd be a centerfold.

"We can be friends!" she says, pushing the dessert into my mouth.

I nod vigorously.

Beside her stands Wilma from the front desk. "It's an old family recipe," she explains to me. "Jupiter aligned with marzipan."

"It's great!" I say, swallowing. "Could I have some more?"

"I can do that!" The girl hastens away.

"Thanks for being so nice to Barbara," Wilma whispers to me. "She's my special child."

"She's your daughter?" I say. "But she doesn't look like . . . I mean she's really . . . nice," I finish, lamely.

Wilma smiles. "She's very special. I cried when she was born, but I'm used to her now. I love her for who she is, poor homely thing."

"Ho-homely?" Remember, Wilma is a myopic frog, squatting waist high and belching cigarette smoke like a factory chimney. I guess it's all a question of context.

"She's so . . . hairy." Wilma shudders. "And her skin is that pasty golden color, and her legs are scrawny."

"Oh, I don't know," I say, staring across the room. Barbara has her back to me. Her legs go right up, and her hair goes right down.

"It's okay, Crime Dog. You already told me you like 'em big. Ho-ho-ho." Wilma stretches her own left leg out. It's as long as she is. She waggles her long webbed toes. "Now *that*'s big," she says.

Two guys hop up to me – one with a cigar and one with a porkpie hat instead of the usual ball cap. "Hey, Crime Dog," says Cigar. "Settle a bet here. Wes and I were arguing about which pitcher you've had the most success against."

Porkpie is Wes, I guess.

I go blank. I cannot recall the name of a single major-league pitcher. Not one. "Grunewald," I say, at length.

They frown at each other. "Grunewald?"

"One game I hit four home runs in a row off him," I say. I don't explain that it was in our backyard, and we were using a beach ball and a tennis racket. Grunewald is my friend Victor's last name.

"Grunewald plays for Cleveland, right?" asks Wes. His porkpie hat is the same pale yellow color as his underbelly.

I try to think how to put it. "I'm pretty sure he's *heard* of Cleveland," I say.

I leave them muttering to each other, and go after Barbara. I find her standing in front of the cake. Here, at Bogway Park Lodge, they do things big. Big toilets, big beds, big cakes. This marzipan thing is like a section of wall, almost as high as the ceiling and as thick as the table it's resting on. Barbara is scooping a piece of the cake onto a plate for me. Beside her, a clutch of little tadpoles are digging in with spoons. An older frog is leaping to the top of the cake to get some icing for her plate.

"Hi, Barbara," I say, coming up behind her. "That's some cake, huh?"

Her legs look perfect.

She turns. "Hi, there!" she says, the same way she did when she first saw me. "Let's be friends!" She seems glad to see me. A beautiful naked girl is glad to see me. All right, maybe that happens to you every day, but it's a new experience for me.

"Uh . . . sure," I say. I swallow. "Sure," I say again.

Smooth, Dingwall, very smooth.

I step forward, with no very definite idea in my mind. Her hand reaches for me. And that's when something heavy crashes into the side of the building.

The frogs stop talking at once. The room waits. "Is it him?" someone whispers.

There it is again. And again. Could it be an earthquake? No. An earthquake doesn't knock like a hammer on the wall of the building. An earthquake doesn't rattle the furniture – no, wait, it does do that. An earthquake doesn't cast a shadow when it crosses in front of a window.

"It's him!" croaks one of the frogs, in a voice loud enough for all to hear. I look over. It's Wes, my friend in the porkpie hat. He's standing a bit farther down the cake, looking nervous. "He's back!"

And panic strikes, as suddenly as diarrhea. One minute it's not there, and the next minute you can't think of anything else. The lobby of the lodge is full of giant leaping frogs. They bound past me on the way to the door, crashing into one another in midair, falling, sprawling, flopping, hopping. The doorway is jammed with slippery green bodies.

Something is pounding on the outside wall, hard enough to shake the whole building. The hysteria mounts. I want to get out, but I can't seem to move my legs. The frogs are everywhere. I'm bigger than they are, but not faster. I can't push them all out of the way. I call for Norbert, but my voice is lost in the thunder of croaking.

And then the building starts to come down. I am curiously calm as I notice the wall nearest me detach itself from the ceiling, and fall towards me. Time slows down. Sound and feeling go away. The wall hits me, silent, painless, heavy, knocking me to the floor. My left arm is pinned beneath me. I scream silently, reach out blindly with my right hand. Then the floor hits me from underneath, and I can feel myself going up like an express elevator. I don't know how long this feeling lasts – not very long. When it stops, everything is quiet.

My mouth is full of something soft and tasty. I swallow instinctively. Almond cake. I can't see. Something is pressing on my eyes. And the rest of me. Something heavy, but bearable, like a dozen blankets. I struggle, but can't lift myself. My left arm has fallen asleep.

"Hello?" I say. When I open my mouth, more almond cake falls in. I chew and swallow. "Hello?" My voice sounds remote from the rest of me, the way it does after your ears have popped.

I can't move any part of me except my mouth and right arm. I feel around blindly. "Help!" I call. More almond cake. I chew and swallow. "Help!" I call again.

Something soft under my fingers. Soft and smooth and rounded. I have no idea what it can be. A water balloon? I squeeze it a bit, and hear a voice I recognize.

"Hi there!"

"Barbara?" I say. "Barbara, are you okay?"

"This is fun!" she says.

More almond cake in my mouth because my mouth is wide open. I think I know what I have my hand on. Not a water balloon.

"Sorry!" I say. I move my hand away from her . . . her. . . .

With the rosy red tidal wave of embarrassment comes a – belated – dawning of sense. I realize that I am not quite as helpless as I feel. It wasn't a real wall that fell on me, but a wall of cake. It's as thick and almost as heavy as stone, but not nearly as strong. I snake my right hand back to my side, and use it to push cake away from my eyes. Some falls into my mouth. I swallow it. I shake my left arm, which is tingling, coming back to life. I can use it. I push some cake out of the way, trying to dig a tunnel to the top. You know those avalanche movies? It's sort of like that. Or *The Great*

Escape. But with one key difference. There isn't any place to put the handfuls of cake I'm clearing away. I can't reach behind me. The only empty space I have is my mouth. I fill it quickly. When I swallow, it's empty again. So I fill it again. And again.

That's right, I end up eating my way to freedom. Handful after handful, bite after bite. Sounds like it'd be fun, but it isn't. For one thing, there's no milk to wash it down. And there's no stopping, even after I begin to get full. My mom calls me a bottomless pit, but I'm not. I'd like to be excused, but I keep eating anyway. I breathe cake. I live cake. My world is cake. I keep chewing and swallowing until there's enough space around me so that I can sit up. That's better. I move faster now, digging through cake like a dog, pushing the handfuls behind me, clawing, scrabbling, tunneling, until, at long last, my hands break through. I clear enough cake away to get my head out, and take a deep breath of air that doesn't reek of almonds. A few frantic after-dinner heaves later and I'm standing in waist-deep cake. I climb out without too much difficulty. My space suit feels too tight, my hair is full of crumbs, and I've eaten enough dessert to last me all the birthdays of my life, but I'm free.

10

Think About It

The lobby of Bogway Park Lodge is deserted, except for me, and Barbara under the cake, and Norbert.

Norbert is sitting on a chair with his hands clasped together. His anxious expression vanishes when he sees me.

– *Well, if it isn't Ding-Dog,* he says.

The night is silent. No more pounding and shaking and screaming. The intruder, whoever he was, seems to be gone.

"Shut up, Norbert," I say, "and help me dig."

– *Buried treasure?*

"Something like that."

He picks his way past a broken coffee table and bits of fallen ceiling. – *I was wondering where you were. I didn't think to look under there.*

The slab of cake is the size of a limousine. I begin digging near the hole I came out of, scooping away handfuls and throwing them behind me. "What happened just now?" I ask. "The frogs knew what was going on. 'It's him,' they said."

Norbert shrugs. – *I didn't see anyone.*

I lift him on top of the cake and tell him to dig down while I dig across. I hope he finds Barbara before I do. I'm a little shy of her.

"Crime Dog!" calls Wilma, from the doorway. "Have you seen my daughter? I can't find her anywhere."

"She's in here," I say, grabbing another handful of cake.

– *Oh ho!* says Norbert. *A booby prize.*

"Very funny," I mutter.

Wilma hops over to help. "Barbara!" she calls. "Barbara, can you hear me?" Behind the glasses, her eyes bulge with a mother's love.

I clear a path into the cake, and reach as far forward as I can. The smell of marzipan sticks in my nostrils. Nothing, and then –

"Ouch!"

Feels like my finger is caught in a mousetrap. I yank hard and out pops Barbara's head – golden hair plastered down, beautiful face covered in crumbs, full-lipped mouth clamped around my index finger. "Hi, there!" she says. "Let's be friends."

I slide out my finger thankfully and Norbert hops down from the cake. We stand back while Wilma sets her daughter free and embraces her. The bog-smelling frog and the beautiful girl seem happy together.

Wilma and Barbara say good-bye to us in the lodge's broken doorway. The night is blue-gray under the moons. The air is dank and buggy. The swamp is as flat as stale cola, and about the same color.

"I'm so sorry you have to go, Crime Dog," she says, over her daughter's head. "You too, Prince Norbert. But I've got no choice. There's nowhere to put you. Usually the monster just makes a bit of a mess, but tonight he took down the whole guest wing."

The monster, it turns out, is a famous feature of the Bogway Park Lodge. There are souvenirs and photographs of him for sale in the gift shop.

"You sure your monster isn't a black giant with a sword and a helmet?" I ask, thinking, of course, of the Dey.

"Oh, no. Our monster's green." Wilma hops forward and puts one smooth hand on my hip. Her fingertips are pale yellow. Her cigarette end glows red as she inhales. "You know, Crime Dog, we'll have this place repaired in a few weeks. Maybe you'd like to come back? Hmmm. . . ." She winks. "Would you like a coupon? One night's free accommodation."

"I, uh, don't know when I'll be traveling this way again," I say.

"Think about it," she says huskily. "Think hard. Bye-bye, now."

She leads her daughter away. I can't help staring after them. Barbara's hair falls down her back like a blonde waterfall. There's a big piece of vanilla icing stuck to her, just below it. Looks just like the bottom half of a bikini.

11

Surprise

Daybreak. The sun has not yet risen, but fingers of pale gold are reaching over the horizon. The sky is still blue-gray under the twin half-moons, the full moon (Sid), and the sliver of a new moon away to my right. Norbert and I are flying quickly. My bathrobe makes flapping noises around my knees.

Wilma, Barbara, Wes, and the rest of the gang at Bogway Fen are way behind us. With Sid on our right, we are now flying over rounded hills that look something like a close-up of my aunt's bedspread. We're looking for the Parietal River.

I say we, but it's really Norbert doing the looking and the finding. I know what a river looks like when I'm swimming in it, or when it's on a map (that is, if it's labeled), but I have no idea what it looks like from fifty stories in the air.

I'm really surprised when Norbert swoops down to chase after a silver-green streak.

I swoop right after him. I'm getting better at swooping. I'm not as fast as Norbert when we're climbing, but I can catch him every time when we're heading down. I crouch low, like a skier, and point my toes and whoosh right past him.

I'm not a bit tired. Too excited, probably. I'm sure not hungry.

Midmorning. The sun hangs above us like a picture, and the Parietal River unwinds below us like a spool of thread. We've been following it for the past two hours through the Random Lands. Now, these are interesting. They're called random from the way the landscape and weather make sudden and inexplicable changes. From minute to minute, you don't know what you're going to get. Right now the river is running quickly down a rocky hillside. Lots of boulders. The air is dry and cool. But just a few minutes ago the river was wide and lazy, and it was raining like Noah.

I keep my eyes peeled for a something called the Amyg Dale. That's where we turn north. I hope Norbert has his eyes peeled too. I have no idea what a dale looks like.

Norbert swings back to fly beside me.

– *Thirsty,* he says. I don't know if he's asking or telling.

"Yes," I say.

He nods, and drops like a stone. There's a tree standing by itself on the banks of our river, just as it makes a bend. The lower branches overhang the flowing water. Norbert lands easily on one of these branches. I follow. The river chuckles away beneath us.

The branch creaks beneath our weight. – *Careful, Dingwall,* he says. *You're a wide load here.*

You know, I could get sick of all these size references.

"Am not," I say.

Standing on the branch, Norbert can bend all the way over at the waist so that his face is just above the surface of water, and his antennae are actually submerged.

– *Ahh. That feels so-o-o-o Sid. I'm still tired from last night.*

I kneel on the branch, lean over, and dip my whole head in the river. Oh, does it feel wonderful! I drink and drink, and come up splashing.

– *Careful, Dingwall!*

We sit there on the branch, resting, restoring. Norbert stands up and puts his hands behind his head. I ask him about the planet's history. "Was there ever a time before the Black Dey?"

He ponders. – *Gee, Dingwall, I really don't know. It's hard for me to imagine him not being here. We don't think about the past much, on Jupiter. So many things are always the same. There's always a Queen Betunka in Betunkaville. And there's always a King Sheldon in Sheldonburg. The moons ride across the sky, and the beaches are warm, and the children learn their times tables. Cocoa is sweet, and cowboys are true, and love is forever. What else do you need? We don't learn history in school because the past is always with us. It's part of our present.*

"And the Black Dey is always there, strong and evil, waiting to carry you away?"

– Uh-huh.

"And you like that?"

– Well, you get used to it.

The river hurries past us, telling itself the stories it has always told. I suppose it's been here since this part of the country was formed, and it's still here. The water's different every second, but the river's the same. Is this what Norbert's getting at?

"So what about me?" I ask him. "Why bring me here to get rid of the Dey if you're used to him? I'm an alien. I'm different. Why go all the way to Earth to find a champion?"

He stares at me. *– The prophecy has always been here too, and you're part of that. We've always tried to fulfill the prophecy.*

"But I haven't always been here."

– Longer than you think.

"What do you mean? I've been here less than a day!"

I can't make him admit he's wrong, so I splash him.

– Cut that out, Dingwall!

"That'll teach you to call me a wide load," I say. I bend down to splash him again. The branch gives a loud crack, and I pitch headfirst into the river.

No worries about drowning; I'm a good swimmer. Under my heavy bathrobe, the space suit is buoyant. I drift with the current. Feetfirst, for safety. The water is flowing faster now.

Norbert flies overhead. I'm on my back, looking up; he's in the air, looking down. A concerned expression on his face.

Surprise

— Are you all right, Dingwall? Do you want help getting out?

"No, thanks," I say. "This is refreshing. Say, am I going in the right direction?"

— You have no idea how wrong the direction is.

"What do you mean?"

I lift my head, but I can't see the river. This puzzles me for a second, and then I understand. There's no more river to see. We've come to a cliff, and the water is falling in a cascade towards a lake below. This is a surprise, all right! I float over the edge of the waterfall, and, for the second time in less than a day, find myself plummeting towards my doom.

12

The End

Falling water all around me. I'm tumbling like a spare sock in the washing machine. This is no good. I spread my arms to straighten myself out, and wiggle my toes. That's better. Now I'm in the air, with the wall of water behind me.

I try to clench my toes, but I can't get a grip in the wet slippers. I don't stop.

It reminds me of trying to brake in wet weather. Riding my bike last summer, I sailed right through a busy intersection on the red light because my brake pads refused to grip. I've never had so many fingers raised at me.

I look down. The ground is coming up fast. It's a beautiful scene. The falling water is so white, and the pool below so blue. There's a beach of golden sand around the pool. As the river continues down the valley, the sand gives way to bright green grass and ferns that overhang the water.

The End

Clench, Dingwall! Clench those delicate pink tootsies! But I can't. They keep slipping. I've got to think of something. Got to . . . wait a minute. I can't clench my toes, but I can wiggle them. Which means I can steer, even if I can't stop.

That's the answer. Got to hurry, though, because I've fallen a long long way and the beautiful blue pool of water is hurtling towards me. Actually, I'm hurtling towards it. I wiggle my toes and point my slippers to the side and slightly up, and *just* before I hit, I think: *I'm too late*. And I am. I smash into the pool and get the wind knocked out of me. I start to sink. What a disappointment! I'm dying on a strange planet with my quest unfulfilled. The hidden castle is still hidden. The villain is flourishing. I've let down my friend and myself. Some champion I am. The water closes over my head.

The End.

13

The Dale

I really thought I was dying. I'm surprised to wake up on the sandy beach with Norbert panting beside me.

The sun peeps over the rim of the cliff. The waterfall looks like a cascade of diamonds. I can hear country music playing in the background. Something about living each day like you were dying. Appropriate, or what? I'm light-headed.

"Is this heaven?" I ask weakly.

Norbert turns towards me, water glistening on his smooth white head. His eyes are crinkled. He's smiling.

– *There's optimism for you! Heaven? What would you be doing in heaven? If there was any justice, Dingwall, I'd be poking you with a pitchfork. Do you know how heavy you are?*

I prop myself up on my elbows. Everything hurts. My stomach muscles hurt. My side hurts. My hair hurts. Actually, my hair hurts a lot. My feet hurt. I feel wonderful.

"You keep telling me that. So I guess you pulled me out of the water?"

– *Uh-huh.*

"Dived in after me and grabbed me before I sank? Pulled me up the beach by my collar?"

– *Actually, by your hair.*

No wonder it hurts. I sit up straight. "Well, thanks, Norbert. Thanks a lot." He looks away. "I mean it," I say.

– *Uh-huh.*

The country singer is going skydiving and rocky mountain climbing. I look around for the radio, and notice a colorful shell. I reach for it.

"Hey! Put that back!"

The voice sounds sort of familiar, dry and grumpy. I turn. A crab stands stiffly, claws poised over his head, eyes out on the end of their stalks. They glare at me.

"Drop the shell!" he says.

"It's pretty," I say.

"Drop it! Drop it at once!"

I turn to Norbert. "He reminds me of the guy in charge of the storeroom in Betunkaville," I say.

– *I know The Jim has a brother somewhere,* says Norbert.

"The Jim?" The little crab waves his claws menacingly over his head. "Who speaks of The Jim? The Jim went away! He didn't think the dale was big enough! Now I am The Dale! The only Dale. Drop the shell, I say! No touching! This dale is mine."

I put down the shell. It is a pretty one: whorls and whirls in a rainbow of color.

"You're looking at the shell!" He scuttles over to it and buries it under the sand. "No looking!"

A different song begins to play. "Free-Falling." I know this one. I start to hum along. The Dale rolls his eyes to the top of their stalks, and scuttles under a little beach umbrella nearby. Blue and white stripes, about the size of a handkerchief. The song stops. I guess he turned off his radio.

"No listening," he calls, from under the umbrella.

I have to fight back a smile. "But now you can't hear the song, either."

"I'll hear it as soon as you leave!"

He's tiny – smaller than my hand – but completely fearless. He walks right up to me. "Go away!" he says, waving his pincers. "Leave the dale. Leave like The Jim, and never come back!"

A stray thought enters my brain by a side door. "Which dale is this?" I ask.

He hesitates. He doesn't want to give anything away, not even information.

"If you tell us where we are," I say, "we'll go. And you can play with your shell, and listen to your radio in peace."

He hesitates. Then, "The Amyg Dale," he says, in a low voice.

Thought so. "Hey, Norbert, isn't the Amyg Dale where we're supposed to turn away from the river?"

"Now, go!" cries the crabby crab.

And we do. I have to wring out my bathrobe and empty the water out of my slippers, but I'm ready to go a lot sooner than you'd think. My hair hurts when I push it out of my eyes. My toes hurt when I wiggle them. But I can fly. My quest is still alive. We fly back up the cliff together, Norbert and I, and head away from the Amyg Dale. Next stop, the Sudden Mountains.

14

Nightingale

The wind is blowing right in my face. My robe and slippers are dry. Actually, I'm fairly dry myself. I wouldn't mind a drink, and maybe something to eat. It's been a while since the cake. A band of cloud cuts across the horizon up ahead. It's moving towards us, pushed by the wind. Lightning plays off to the right. Norbert is just behind me and we're flying fairly low to the ground.

"Do you know where the Sudden Mountains are?" I call to him.

He shakes his head. – *We're a couple hours from the Amyg Dale, so the mountains should be nearby. But I don't know exactly where.*

"Should we ask for directions?"

– *Dingwall, these are the Random Lands. Sudden forests, sudden deserts, sudden mountains. Look down right now. Go on, look as hard as you like. What do you see? Rocks. Want to ask a handful of pebbles for directions?*

"I see a road," I say.

– Where?

I point to a ribbon of gray cutting through the stones. It leads over behind a hill on our left. "Come on," I say. "The road will lead us to civilization – a place where we can ask directions and find some breakfast."

– Wait, Dingwall! he cries.

But I'm thinking about breakfast. I follow the gray ribbon around the hill with Norbert on my tail, calling me names, telling me to slow down, that he doesn't trust the weather or the road, that there might be minions around.

What a worrier!

By the time we get to the other side of the hill, I realize that the bank of cloud is closer than I thought. In fact, it's right here, a rounded billow of white reaching from the sky to the ground. The road disappears into it, like a snake going under a lady's long skirt. I point it out to Norbert.

"We could head down," I say. "Maybe there's a restaurant."

Norbert snorts. *– A restaurant? Why stop there? Maybe there's a movie theater. Maybe there's a hotel, with a hot tub in every room. Or a candy mine, with bucketfuls of raw jujubes.*

"Don't be silly. There's no such thing as a candy mine. Not even on Jupiter. Is there?" I say. Mind you, come to think of it, Jupiter is exactly the sort of place where there might be a candy mine. Hmmm. I wonder what raw jujubes would taste like. "What's your favorite color of jujube?" I ask. "Mine's black."

– *Dingwall, there's no mine down there. There's nothing. The road doesn't go anywhere.*

"Then why build it?" I ask.

– *Why, indeed?*

And the mist covers us. The air is suddenly cooler. I pull my bathrobe tight around me, and keep flying until I feel a gentle bump against my chest and hear a faint beautiful *wheet wheet* sound. I've flown into a bird.

I exclaim, and stop.

– *What now?* asks Norbert.

"Sorry," says the bird, in a musical flutey voice. It seems to be stuck in my robe. I pull it free. A small brown bird with smooth wings and bright red eyes.

"Sorry," it says again. "You must hate me for running into you."

"Not at all," I say. "I ran you down."

"No, it's my fault! I feel horrible. My heart aches, and a drowsy numbness pains my senses. As if of hemlock I had drunk, or drained some dull opiate to the drains."

"That bad, eh?" I say. "You should eat something."

The bird introduces herself as Jenny. She's not shy. "As a matter of fact, I was on my way to the mill for breakfast, when I got lost in the fog," she says.

"There's a mill near here? With a restaurant?"

"Sure. A good restaurant. Five stars. I go there all the time. It's easy to find. Just follow the road. Want to come with me?"

I sure do! "Sounds good, hey, Norbert?"

– *Hmph.*

"I told you that road went somewhere."

– *How come you got lost if the mill's so easy to find?* he asks her. He sounds suspicious.

"I told you, it was the fog."

Just then a gust of wind blows the fog clear for a moment, and I catch sight of rising rocky ground, with a ribbon of road snaking ahead.

"There's the road!" I cry out. "We'll go with you, Jenny. Then you won't be blown off course again." She perches on my finger, and sings her thanks. What a nice bird. "You're some kind of sparrow, I guess," I say.

"Sparrow?" For a second, I hear iron in her voice. Then she softens it again. "I'm a light-wingèd Dryad of the trees." She sings a few liquid warbling phrases. "That selfsame song was heard by Ruth when, sick for home, she stood alone amidst the alien corn," she says.

"Oh," I say.

The cloud bank covers us again, thicker than before. It's like flying through mushroom soup. I can't see ahead. Not a block, not a stone's throw, not a car length. I hold out my own hand. It disappears into a thick wall of white mist.

– *Slow down!* cries Norbert, grabbing my arm.

I stop moving my toes. We're barely moving. That's when I hear a strange sound dead ahead. *Creak . . . creak creak.* What is it?

A gust of wind hits from my left side. I heel like a sailing ship in a storm, barely able to keep my balance. Then, without warning, the wind veers and attacks from behind.

– *I don't like this,* says Norbert.

No use in staring ahead. I can't see past my nose. I fly slowly, and listen hard.

There it is again.

Creak . . . creak creak . . . creak creak. It's regular, and mechanical. The cloud bank swirls away for a second and shows a triangular sail, which disappears into the mist, and then reappears in the same place. Then it disappears and reappears again. And I realize it's not the same sail. Four sails going round and round.

Jenny gives a charming throaty laugh. "That's the mill, silly," she says.

"What's it doing in midair?" I ask.

We fly closer. Of course, the windmill is not in midair, but on a little outcrop of bare rock. The ground drops steeply away from the mill, and rises steeply beside it.

"It's a mountain!" I say. "See that? The rock goes straight up. Where'd that mountain come from? Wow! It popped right out of the cloud like a jack-in-the-box!"

– *That's why they call these the Sudden Mountains,* says Norbert.

"Good thing we were going slowly. If we'd been flying at a normal speed, we'd have crashed into them."

The mountainside is sheer and jagged, like a giant steak knife pointing at the sky. The mill perches precariously.

"Let's go inside," says Jenny. "I wonder what they've got on the menu today. I'm kind of thirsty, aren't you? I could really go for a draught of vintage that hath been cool'd a long age in the deep-delvèd earth, Tasting of Flora and the country-green, dance, and Provençal song, and sunburnt mirth!"

"Sure," I say, "that sounds pretty good."

Creak. Creak creak. The windmill has blue sides, a white top, and red sails. It looks very familiar. I fly closer, and find out why. My dad and I put together one just like it. This was before the divorce, when I was small. I couldn't help much. Dad got down on his hands and knees on the living room floor, hunting for different-sized plastic pieces, and cursing the manufacturer.

"Hey, Norbert!" I call. He's behind me. "The mill looks like it's made out of those snap-together bricks."

– What? Get back, Dingwall! Get back at once! That's a proteor.

"A what?"

– It's another of the Black Dey's minions! It can make itself look like anything. Where's that blasted bird?

I feel Jenny crawling up my bathrobe. "Ah, youth," she mutters to me, "that grows pale, and spectre thin, *and dies!*" She breaks out in a strange thin nasty laugh. Quite unlike her. I look down and –

"Ugh!"

I freeze, clenching my toes in instinctive horror. A large brown spider with Jenny's bright red eyes is crawling across my bathrobe, cackling to herself. Like the windmill, she's made of plastic bricks. I can see where they snap together to make her long jointed legs. I guess she was made of plastic bricks when she was a bird too. That's the great thing about those bricks: you can turn them into whatever you like.

The windmill, for instance, has turned into a circular saw, complete with a rotating sharp blade.

Jenny, thrown from me when I stop dead, ends up underneath the saw blades.

Norbert grabs my arm and pulls me away. A soft, kindly blanket of cloud wraps itself around us. I don't know if the saw can see us, but I can't see it.

– *Come on, Dingwall,* says Norbert.

"Which way?"

– *We've got to get over the mountains, right? So I'd suggest up.*

I try to smile, but I'm still shaken. "Jenny was a spider," I say, in a small voice.

– *No, she wasn't.* Norbert is firm. *She was a bunch of little plastic blocks. By now, she's something else. Think of her as a car, or a chair. Or a window frame. Hard to be scared of a window frame, isn't it?*

I almost smile. "You never liked her, did you? How come?"

– *Maybe I'm scared of little plastic blocks.*

15

Too Much Distance

We angle our slippers upward and begin to climb. My calf muscles remind me that I had to stretch them like this yesterday afternoon, climbing out of the Chasm near Betunkaville. We keep climbing. We take a zigzag route across the face of the mountain, counting to a hundred and then angling back the way we came. My world is narrow: the dwarfish clingy mosses and steeply angled sweating rocks in front of me, and Norbert's slippers above. When we take a moment to catch our breath, I look around. Thick curls of mist obscure where we've been, and where we still have to go.

We keep climbing.

And climbing.

And that's it for a while. We climb, and get blown backward and forward by gusts of wind, and climb some more, and try to keep a sharp lookout for snap-together enemies. As we climb higher, I find that my body gets more tired but my mind becomes more active.

Altitude, I realize, is more than distance from the ground; it's also distance from all things relating to the ground. I feel this within me as I climb higher and higher. I feel my body becoming less and less important to me. My mind ranges wide and high over all that I know, all my experience, analyzing, judging from a great height. I understand and appreciate more than I ever have, and I worry less.

I consider the phenomenon of the mountains suddenly popping out at me from behind the cloud cover. Sudden Mountains, indeed. An excellent name. Very apt.

I consider the phenomenon of the sail on a windmill. It traps the wind going one direction, and utilizes it in another. A matter of forces and vectors. Fascinating.

I consider my loneliness. I'm an only child. I've been lonely most of my life. The reason Norbert and I get along so well is that we're company for each other.

I consider Jenny's trickery, and why it bothers me. It isn't that she was bad. (I've been in the same class as Mary the bully since kindergarten. I've seen girls behave badly.) No, it's the fact that Jenny started out nice and then turned into a nightmare. Treachery. That's the scary thing. Not the spider, but the bird turning into the spider.

I consider the Dey's castle. The Lost Schloss. Now, that's hard to think, let alone say. Lost Schloss. Lost Schloss. Losht Slosh. Loscht Schloscht. I sound like I'm drunk.

Schloshed. I giggle. I wonder where the Schloss can be schituated? How do you hide something on a plain? A plain is flat, and a schloss is, well, pointy.

I keep climbing. I'm thirsty. I feel as though I've been climbing forever. I wonder what time it is, what day it is.

I catch up to Norbert. This climbing is hard on him. He's braver and smarter than I am, but not nearly as strong. His eyes are almost shut. His antennae are flat on the top of his head.

"Come on, Norbert," I say, pushing him upward. His feet point all over the place, making it difficult. "Keep going. It's not too far now." This doesn't feel like a lie because I really have no idea how far it is. For all I actually *know*, I might be telling the truth.

He mutters to himself. – *Hang on, Nerissa,* he says. *We're coming.*

I keep climbing. My legs and feet hurt. And I'm so-o-o-o thirsty.

Soon it's clear that Norbert can't go on. I put him on my back, with his arms over my shoulders. I keep climbing, carrying him piggyback. "We're nearly there," I tell him.

And we are. I just don't know where *there* is.

He falls asleep and begins muttering to himself, having imaginary conversations with Nerissa. – *Sorry I'm late,* he says. *It's all Dingwall's fault.*

I can feel Norbert's head swaying back and forth as I make the switchbacks. He snores gently, like a little kid taking a nap. Poor guy, he's totally worn-out.

I keep climbing. The rocks have frost and snow on them now. The mist is getting thinner. It can't be much farther, can it?

Norbert starts talking about me. – *You know what I don't like about Dingwall?* he says. *He's too negative.*

He must think he's talking to Nerissa. "You know, I'm right here," I say.

– *No, no. Don't defend him. You don't really know him. I know Dingwall, and he's the biggest Gloomy Gus you'll ever meet. Always ready to fail. Always ready to back out. If only Dingwall knew how much he has going for him, he'd . . .*

"I'd what?" I say, but Norbert has drifted off again.

The climbing seems to be easier. It's almost like floating upwards on the wind. The higher I climb, the less I feel like doing. I'd rather observe life, smiling with infinite understanding, infinite patience, infinite tolerance. I feel like a feather, or a dandelion seed, or a balloon. Except that my feet are killing me.

The mist remains thick below us, but thins to nothing as I look up. The sky overhead is almost clear.

I see a splash of green on the mountainside – the first sign of life.

– *Know what else I don't like about Dingwall?* says Norbert suddenly.

I look back over my shoulder. His eyes are shut. His head lolls. He's fast asleep.

– *Low self-esteem. Dingwall should like himself more.*

"Well, you're not helping," I say.

– I think he's great. He's funny, and creative. He's a good friend.

"I am? I mean, he is?"

– He doesn't have anything to be scared of. But he is scared. He should let himself go more. Be free. He should realize that who he is is okay. He doesn't have to worry about anything. Oh, except for the nose picking. That's gross! Once last week, he almost totalled my kitchen. Flakes of plaster falling from the ceiling, and this giant –

"Hey!" I say. I wiggle my shoulders from side to side. I don't have to listen to this.

As I reach the mountaintop, the mist evaporates. It's clear, cool, and just past dawn. Looking into the distance, I can see the top half of a yellow disc shining palely.

Sunrise. It's a new day. I wonder what happened to the old one. We must have been climbing all night.

My feet need a rest. I fly over to a flat rock and land awkwardly, with Norbert's weight on my back. I put him down, and drop to my knees. A cup-sized hollow in the middle of the rock contains snowmelt. I drink from my hands. The water is cool and sharp tasting. I splash some on my face, then on Norbert's. He wakes up, groaning.

A creature rears up out of a nearby snowdrift. It's as big as a car, with a single eye staring from the top of its box-shaped head, and a single arm sticking straight out from its body like a crane. I can see the bumps and hollows of snap-together pieces. This is another proteor.

A cage hangs from the end of the proteor's arm. It's a

colorful box with bars – the kind of cage that holds lions and tigers in the old circus movies. The proteor lowers the cage to the ground, and I see that there's something inside. I wonder what lives in the Sudden Mountains.

The long arm has a hook on the end. It swings towards me in a flash, and the hook catches the belt of my bathrobe. The crane hoists me in the air.

– *Oh, no!* cries Norbert.

It's a strong belt, made of good thick toweling. I'm hooked, all right. The arm of the crane ratchets in a series of clicks.

Norbert flies over and tears at the hook, yelling at me to do something. I'm philosophical. The proteor's stronger than I am. I guess this is how things are supposed to work out. It's destiny. What can you do?

The proteor gives off a faint smell of lubricating oil. Not unpleasant.

The cage is just below me now. When I see the animal inside, I almost choke.

Norbert is surprised too. – *Would you look at that! I thought they were all gone.*

A puppy-sized animal, with vibrant gold and crimson stripes. A familiar animal, with pointy ears and a long nose and handles sticking out of its neck. A scared animal, round eyes rolling, trembling legs fitted into two curved wooden rails.

A horse. A rocking horse. My rocking horse.

"Barnaby?" I call down to it, in a gentle voice. "Barnaby, is that you?"

16

Mr. Proteor

I remember my rocking horse vividly, my favorite plaything until I got too big. I kept him at the foot of my bed, and I loved him more than anything else in the world.

Here on Jupiter, he's alive and trapped in a cage by a snap-together monster. He looks up when he hears his name. I know he can understand me. My heart swells like a wet sponge. I care about him. I really do. I feel so bad for him.

"We've got to save him!" I cry. I forget about fate and free will and things working out the way they do. I cannot let Barnaby be taken to the Black Dey, and broken. I cannot.

I'm right above the cage now, close enough to see how the door works. Barnaby rocks himself over to where I am, and whickers softly and very horsily. The appeal in his eyes is like a hook in my heart.

"Norbert," I whisper. "I want you to distract the proteor while I get Barnaby out."

– How are you going to do that? You're hooked.

"Just do it, okay? Talk to him. You're a great talker. I need only thirty seconds or so. Ready? Go!"

Norbert called me a good friend. He's a good friend too. Even before I finish my sentence he's in the air, talking loudly. Sounds like he's pretending to be an image consultant.

*– So let me ask you this, Mr. Proteor: what were you think-*ing *when you put yourself together this morning? Did you even look in the mirror? Because you left the house with only one eye. Do you know that? Have you noticed a lack of depth perception? I thought so. Dear, dear. You're going to have to pay more attention to yourself, Mr. Proteor. A little more* you *time, if you understand me. Oops! Careful there.*

I check over my shoulder. Norbert is hovering near the box part of the crane. The proteor flails its crane arm across, narrowly missing him. Norbert keeps talking.

– And I want to talk to you very frankly about your choice of shape. . . .

I can't pull the hook out of my bathrobe belt, but I can untie the knot at the front. The ends of the belt fall, and the hook comes loose. I drop to the ground, landing gently in the snow. I run to the cage, slide open the latch, and reach for Barnaby. He struggles. He is a wild rocking horse, after all. But he's not heavy. I gather him into my arms and hold him tight.

"Sorry, Barnaby," I whisper. "I'm so sorry!"

He nuzzles me in the neck. His striped fur is soft and silky. His nostrils are pink and smooth. His heart beats loudly against my chest.

Time to go. I take a step and fall to the ground. Boy, does that hurt!

Barnaby leaps from my arms and stands nearby, quivering with fear.

I can't believe it. My foot's in a trap. A great big one, with jagged jaws and a spring. The trap is made of yellow and blue snap-together bricks, just like Barnaby's cage, which is . . . gone. Oh, oh. That was a fast transformation. What'll I do?

Lying on the ground full length, I cast around for something to break the proteor's snap-together bonds and free myself. All I find are rocks. I keep looking.

I hear Norbert's voice.

– *I really think you'd do best to take yourself apart and start again. You're a proteor, right? Right? So you can be anything. Honestly, cranes with hooks are so last season. Windmills are even worse. Everyone remembers their windmill years. Now, are you a ladies' man at all, Mr. Proteor? You are? I thought so. You want the ladies to notice you? Sure you do. Well, here's a tip. . . .*

Another rock. I try again. My hands close on a heavy piece of metal. It's rusted, but unmistakable. A sword hilt. I pull it towards me. The sword rings on the stones. I wonder how it got here. Some knight or warrior must have climbed to the top of the Sudden Mountains and fallen in battle to a proteor, leaving his weapon behind for me.

Whoever he was, he was awfully big for a jupiterling. My hand fits the hilt perfectly. The sword feels nicely balanced in my grasp.

A friendly weapon. I don't know how else to put it. My right hand tingles. It's like the sword is saying, *Hi, there. I've been waiting for you!*

I've never held a real sword before, let alone a used one. Good thing it isn't complicated, like a computer or a car. The manual for our computer is 400 pages long. The typical sword manual would be a lot shorter:

(1) *Swing hard.*

(2) *Cut enemy in half.*

(3) *Repeat. Battle cry optional.*

You'd get the whole thing on one page, even if you put the instructions in twenty languages.

Of course, if you make a mistake with a computer, you can just press the undo key. There's no undo key on a sword. If you miss your stroke and, say, cut off your own leg – well, that's permanent. Get used to hopping.

I'm afraid of cutting my leg off. I sit up straight, and lift the sword over my head. Gosh, it's heavy. I close my eyes, and let it fall.

17

Say It with Showers

What a noise it makes! Like a blacksmith's hammer striking the anvil. I open my eyes. The trap is in two wriggling pieces on the ground. The rock is chipped.

I'm free!

"Hey!" I cry aloud. The sword flashes excitement into me. This is a seriously powerful weapon. I mean, I wasn't even trying, and I cut right into the mountain.

I lift the sword, and strike again, and again. Take that, you stupid trap! The pieces split into more pieces. Two more chips appear in the rock. The sword itself is undamaged. It may be my fancy, but it seems lighter, as if it's happy to be used again, after all these years of lying on the mountainside rusting.

The pieces on the ground look like bugs. Nasty wriggling things. I slash at them in a frenzy, chopping them into smaller and smaller pieces. The air fills with a hissing sound, like ice cubes popping.

– *Hey, Dingwall,* cries Norbert, from over my shoulder. *Stop playing with Excalibur. You can't kill a proteor by chopping it up; you can only make more of them. We've got a minute while the big guy's transforming. Let's get going!*

I take a step back. I can feel the sweat running down my body, under my space suit and bathrobe. The little things are wriggling in the snow. I kick at them in disgust.

Norbert's right. It's time to go. The crane is now a heap of wriggling bricks. They're turning into something, though. Something rectangular, with a handle on the short side. I don't want to wait and find out what it is.

I loop the belt of my bathrobe around the sword, and tie it on. I'm bringing it with me. Finally, I have a weapon. A good one, too.

Barnaby looks up at me with his big round eyes. He hasn't moved more than arm's length from me since I pulled him out of the cage. I'd feel so bad if I left him on the mountain with the proteor. And I feel bad enough about him already. "Come here, boy," I say, kneeling down. He trots over. I pick him up and leap into the air. My slippers do the rest.

Norbert darts a quick interested look at the rocking horse under my arm, but doesn't say anything. He's watching the heap of bricks with a smile on his face and his antennae perked forward eagerly.

– *Hey, the big guy is following my fashion advice,* he says.

"What'd you tell him he should turn into?"

He coughs. – *A toaster.*

I peer down. He's right. It's a giant two-slice toaster. Each slice of bread would be about the size of a door.

Barnaby struggles in my arms. I almost drop him, managing to grab him by the neck before he falls. And then he . . . well, relieves his discomfort. "Relieves" is the word, all right. I don't know if you've ever seen a horse relieve his discomfort, but it's pretty spectacular. My grandma used to sing a song about someone named Jeannie with the light brown hair, flowing like a river in the soft summer air. That's Barnaby, only it isn't his hair that's flowing.

It all lands on the proteor. Barnaby keeps going, producing a full and steady stream of . . . well, a full and steady stream.

– *Look out!* cries Norbert.

The proteor is attacking. A huge piece of plastic toast flies out of the slot, heading right for us. I dodge out of the way, keeping Barnaby pointed in the right direction. The toast missile falls to the ground. I aim Barnaby at the open slot.

He's amazing. Like the bunny on TV, he keeps going, and going, and –

– *Smoke!* cries Norbert.

I peer down. A wisp of black is leaking from the heart of the toaster. Something's gone wrong with the mechanism. "Good for you, Barnaby," I say.

It feels good to hit back at the proteor. A personal message. *Say it with showers.*

The smoke gets thicker and darker. Something is burning. The snap-together pieces begin to melt. From up here I can see the bumps and dimples disappear, the straight edges blur and warp. No more transforming for them. There's a loud grinding noise, and one side of the toaster collapses. Norbert and I cheer.

Barnaby's finished. I tuck him under my arm, and fly down the far side of the mountain. The slope is gentle and easy. The wind is gusty, driving a fleet of clouds across the sky like so many purple-gray battleships. Sun and moons peep from behind the clouds, and then disappear behind them again.

Lightning crackles ahead of us, and thunder follows close by. This would have been important to the Ancient Greeks, who believed there were spirits everywhere.* I'm more concerned about getting rained on.

It doesn't take us long to reach a plateau – high flat tablelands that stretch into the distance without a break. A sea of grass rippling in the wind.

"Welcome to the Plains of Ich," says Norbert.

Barnaby is no part of the ancient prophecy. I decide to let him go. But when I release him on the grassy plain, he

---

* Naiads and Dryads, for instance, were nymphs said to inhabit waters and trees. Other nymphs included Whyads and Paiads, who inhabited interrogative sentences and baked goods. Lemon Meringue Paiads were especially beautiful. For more information on classical mythology, see chapter 12: "Our Friends the Greeks."

stands there, looking at me. "Good-bye," I say. "There's a little pond here, and grass. Have a nice life!"

He doesn't move. I shoo him away. He moves closer, and nuzzles my thigh.

Norbert is drinking from the pond. He comes back, wiping his face, looks at me and Barnaby, and doesn't say anything. After a moment I put the horse under my arm and take off again. Norbert follows me. I ask which direction we should head, and he shrugs his shoulders.

– *It's your show now, Dingwall,* he says.

18

The Knights of Ich

It's a couple of hours later, and we haven't come very far in a straight line. I've been leading us all around the compass trying to avoid the storm, but I can't get the wind to stay at our backs for any length of time. The path of the storm seems to veer with us, so that there's lightning wherever we are headed.

I haven't found the Lost Schloss.

Not a sniff of it. Not close. The Schloss has got to be a big building, but I haven't even found a little building. I haven't found the Lost Bungalow. I haven't found the Lost Tent.

I'm not worried. I figure it doesn't really matter where I look for the Schloss. An orderly search is great if you know all about what you're looking for, but I'm looking for something only I can find. So it's all about me. If I'm supposed to fulfill the prophecy, I will. I'll find the castle when it springs from the ground, or falls from the sky, or materializes out of thin air. Or when it turns up on the horizon.

The weather is exciting: wind and dark clouds up close; thunder, lightning, and rain in the distance. But the Plains of Ich are a mere flat infinity of waving grass, an unbroken disc of green stretching to all horizons, a front lawn for Insurance Nation. At this point I'd welcome the sight of a pile of dog poop just to break the tedium. I feel like an ant in the Astrodome.

We fly on. And on. I turn left, and left again. The horizon doesn't change. And then it does. I slow down and squint.

The deep purple clouds overhead part for an instant, so that a single shaft of light can drop like a fly ball into the middle of the landscape. It looks adventitious. At least, I think it does. Maybe I mean advantageous. Or truculent. I've never been sure what truculent means, but it sounds great.* Anyway, what I'm saying is that I notice this pop fly of light not only for its truculentness, but also because it glints off of something.

"Hey, Norbert!" I say, pointing.

There it is again. Another glint. I alter my course, shifting Barnaby under my left arm like a football. He's not much bigger than a football anyway. With difficulty, I draw

---

* truc-u/lent (proposition). 2. A point in English common law, specific to borrowed vehicles. By invoking the truculent clause, the borrower disclaims all knowledge of the vehicle in question, as in, "Gee, Harry, I don't know what happened to the truc-u-lent me." See *adventitious*.

my new sword. I don't want to be caught by surprise. The weapon feels warm and alive in my hand.

"Look ahead, Norbert. Tell me what you see."

He frowns, pauses. – *I see a settled land, under a strong king. I see a beautiful youth with a secret sorrow. I see children playing in a golden afternoon. I see treachery and murder, and the land in ruins. Then, for some reason, I see a tennis racket, and the six of clubs.*

"Very funny," I say. "What I meant was, do you see the knights up ahead? The sun glinted on their armor a minute ago."

– *Yes, Dingwall. They're sitting down at a picnic table, eating and drinking. Their hair is the color of straw, and their mustaches fly in the wind like banners. There's a lake behind them.*

My mouth fills with water at the thought of food. "Do you think they'd let us eat something too?"

– *There's enough on the table for an army! Anyway, they have no weapons that I can see. And they're waving at us.*

By the time we get there they are on their feet, waving and calling cheerful greetings. As Norbert said, they have blonde hair and enormous mustaches.

I stop worrying. These guys are obviously friendly. And they're real people, not proteors. I put away my sword as they crowd around me. They're not too much smaller than I am. For Jupiter, they're pretty big.

"Pleased to meet you, flying travelers," calls the biggest knight, in a voice of brass. He comes up to my chin.

"We've been expecting you. My name is Mount, and I am a knight of Ich."

"Pleased to meet you, Sir Mount," I say, bowing clumsily. "My name is Dingwall and I come from Earth. These are my friends: Prince Norbert of Betunkaville, and Barnaby, a rocking horse."

Sir Mount salutes Norbert and strokes Barnaby's head. He introduces the other knights, who turn out to be his brothers. Their names are Vey, Mise, and Prise. Mise and Prise are twins.

"How do you do," I say. "Sir Vey, Sir Mise, Sir Prise." Vey has bulbous staring eyes, Mise has a long thin nose that crooks a little to the side, Prise has tufted eyebrows that point up all the time. They say they're pleased to meet me. They have English accents, like all the knights I've ever seen or heard of. They say "what" a lot, even when it doesn't mean anything. Kind of the way I say "kind of."

"Sit down, what?" says Sir Prise. "You must be hungry."

"Yes, yes," says Sir Mise. "When I was a boy, I was always hungry. Still am, what?" with a laugh.

"What what?" say the others.

It's hard to take them seriously. Remember the uncle who used to throw you into the air when you were a kid? Who jumped into the pool with a loud splash, so that your mom shook her head? These guys are kind of like him – slightly alarming, but nice.

They have incredible mustaches. Sir Prise's is my favorite: a thick growth all over his cheeks, spreading almost up to his eyes. He looks like he's peering at you through a window in an ivy-covered wall.

"What do you mean, you were expecting us?" I say.

Sir Mount blinks, as though I've asked a stupid question. "I don't know how else to put it," he says. "We knew you had landed. We heard about your quest. We thought you'd come here. We *expected* you, what?" He nibbles at a raw carrot. Yuck.

Norbert and I sit down at a table the size of a tennis court. It's full of all of my favorite foods: fresh oranges and smoked sausages, fried peppers and cabbage rolls, spaghetti and meatballs, spareribs and corn on the cob, kung pao chicken and vindaloo curry, and taffy tarts. There are mountains of peanuts, fields of oatmeal cookies, forests of black licorice, and oceans of chocolate milk. There's more than that, but I don't have time to notice. I reach out greedily, filling my hands, my plate, my mouth.

– *Careful, Dingwall,* says Norbert quietly.

"Something more to drink, boy?" asks Sir Prise kindly. He's sitting next to me.

"Yes, please."

"Oy, down there!" he shouts. "Oy, Vey, pass the cold cocoa for our guest."

Norbert sits up eagerly. – *There's cocoa?*

"Oy, yourself," says Sir Vey. He passes the cocoa. I notice that he's got a carrot going too.

"Ahh, that was good," I say, putting down my glass. "Now, you knights say you know my quest. Can you help me with it? I really want to find the Lost Schloss."

The knights look at each other across the table. Eyebrows and mustaches are hard at work. Sir Mount takes the floor. "I think we can offer our mingled congratulations and condolences, boy," he says.

"That's like good news and bad news, right?"

"The good news is that you stand at the gates of the Lost Schloss."

I look around. I can't see it. Is it invisible? Are they making a joke?

"Okay, what's the bad news?"

Sir Mount raises an ironic eyebrow. "I think it only sporting to tell you that, when you have finished eating, you will have to fight us," he says.

"Hear him!" says Sir Vey, nodding vigorously, so that the ends of his mustache bounce up and down like a cheerleader's pom-poms. "Hear him."

"You see, boy," explains Sir Prise, "we are the guardians of the Lost Schloss. Our lord and master is called the Black Dey of Ich. This is his food you are eating."

Lightning flashes off to the right.

Norbert squeaks in dismay, spilling his cocoa.

I leap to my feet. I can't tell you how stupid I feel. I still don't see any kind of castle. I'll have to look later, though. The knights are on their feet, too, brandishing their carrots at me.

19

Not Peas but a Sword

Yes, I said carrots. They've been nibbling away at the ends, flattening and shaping the carrots with their teeth so that now they look like . . . well, like knives. Big orange knives full of vitamin A.

I don't like raw carrots. When I was little, my mom used to peel one and put it – whole – on my plate beside the Kraft Dinner, or spaghetti, or meat loaf, or whatever, and then she and Dad would go out and leave me with the baby-sitter, who would always insist that I eat the carrot before I could watch TV or play. It might take me the whole evening to choke it down.

Funny, since everything else on this table is food I love, that there should be a plate of raw carrots, and that they should be used as swords against me. I don't understand what's going on, but it's clear what I have to do. I pull out my own sword.

"Do you *want* to fight me?" I ask Sir Mount.

"No, of course not. You're a charming young man. But we serve the Dey, what? We are honorable men. He ordered us to guard the door to the Lost Schloss. So we will guard it. WITH OUR LIVES!" He waves his carrot in the air. "Come on, now, boy. Let's see what you're made of, what?"

"Yah! What?" cry the other knights. They brandish their carrots too.

It's ridiculous, of course. I'm bigger than they are, and I have a real sword.

"Have at you!" Sir Prise surprises me, leaping past his brothers, with his arm outstretched. The pointy end of the carrot is coming right at me. I take careful aim with my sword, and slice the end off his carrot just as another flash of lightning lights up the sky. The thunder is pretty close behind.

He gasps, and stumbles back to the table. There's one of those curved horn of plenty things near his plate. Fruit spilling out of the end. Sir Prise grabs it, and holds it upside down. Plums and peaches come rolling out. He brandishes the empty thing in the air. It looks like a megaphone. Is he going to use it as a weapon? Not a great attack weapon, the megaphone.

– *Behind you, Dingwall!* Norbert is in the air, keeping his eye on the battle.

I turn swiftly. Sir Vey is circling around me. I don't want to hurt him, but I don't want him jumping me either. Sir Mise begins moving the other way. Now there's a knight on either side of me, and I have to move quickly. I fake a lunge at Sir Vey, who backs up, then I spin sideways and slice off most of Sir Mise's carrot. He falls backward, arms in the air like a diver. I don't wait for him to hit the grass. I run back to Sir Vey, who is charging hard. I sidestep, and swing down. Before you can say *What's up, Doc?* his carrot – an extra long one – is gone too.

The score is: sword 3, carrots 0.

"What about you?" I ask Sir Mount. Sweat and rainwater in my eyes; I wipe it away. I'm panting a bit from running back and forth. "You want a piece of this?" I hold out my sword. He counters with his carrot. I take the end off it with a backhanded slash. He's left holding an orange stub. The sword tingles happily in my hand.

Sir Prise holds the narrow end of the horn of plenty up to his mouth. He blows the riff the organist plays at the ball game when the hitting star – say, Fred McGriff – steps up to the plate. You know the one: *da da da DAH, da DAH.* The brothers cheer. He blows it again, the pitch slightly higher: *de de de DEE, de DEE.* And another cheer. And then . . . nothing.

We wait. The thunder growls. Norbert lands beside me. "What now?" I ask him.

– *Don't ask me. Like I said, this is your show.*

Barnaby, who is rocking on the bank of the reedy lake, lets out a sudden high-pitched whinny of fear. We race over, arriving just as a big guy in a black helmet charges up out of the lake and stands on the bank, panting. He looks as though he's run downstairs to answer the doorbell.

"What's wrong now?" he calls. His voice is muffled by the helmet.

"Hi, Dey!" cries Sir Mount.

"Hi, Dey!" cries Sir Vey.

"Hi, Dey!" cry Sir Mise and Sir Prise together.

"Hi," says the big guy.

Norbert nudges me. – *I think that's the Dey,* he whispers.

So this is my opponent – the reason why I'm here. I study him carefully. He's a big one, all right, taller than I am with the helmet, and at least as broad. On Jupiter that makes him a giant. The helmet is the kind the knights used to wear, flat on the top, with slits to see out of and breathe through. It's black, and covers his head completely. His cloak is black too, and goes down to his feet.

His sword is a beauty – straight and heavy like mine, only his is shiny – and he's got a scabbard to keep it in. When he turns quickly to face me, his cloak swirls around him. The rest of his outfit is black too – a shirt with puffy sleeves, tight pants, high button boots. It's all pretty cool, I guess.

He stands in the wings of the storm, ready to fight. His knees are bent. He holds the sword lightly.

It's pointed at me.

"Who the hell are you?" he cries. His eyes flash behind the slits in his helmet. A tough guy.

"This is Dingwall, sir," explains Sir Mount. "He's the boy from Earth."

"Ah, yes! Dingwall." He spits out of the mouth slit in the helmet. I bet he's practised that. "You are the earthling trying to fulfill the ancient prophecy. We've been expecting you. Are you ready to meet your . . . doom?"

On the word "doom," the thunder booms.

— *You look like you're wearing a lampshade on your head,* says Norbert.

The knights look shocked. I smile. The Dey's helmet does look like a black metallic version of the shade from the reading lamp in our living room.

He straightens up. "I know you, little elf," he says. "You're the prince from Betunkaville."

— *Who are you calling an elf, you overgrown . . .*

The wind whips his words away.

"Don't forget, little elf, that I have your princess inside," the Dey reminds Norbert, who stops talking for a full three seconds. He's so mad he can't finish a sentence.

— *Why, you . . . you . . . you . . .* He's fizzing, like a half-opened can of soda pop. *You better not hurt her. If she's hurt, I'll . . . I'll . . .*

"You'll do nothing. I am all that is powerful on this planet."

Lightning flashes behind the Dey as he speaks. Good timing.

I'm thinking hard. *You stand at the gates of the Lost Schloss,* said Sir Mount. The castle must be nearby, but I can't see it. Not a turret, not a tower, not a single stone.

In plain sight, and yet none can see. I don't get it. I don't get it.

"Now, Dingwall, prepare to meet your doom!" The Dey flourishes the sword, sweeping it back and forth, like he's buttering a giant piece of bread. The knights gather round him.

Sir Mount is nibbling on a new carrot. His brothers are already re-armed and ready. "Hear him!" they cry. "You are doomed!" Sir Mise twists his mustache, which is drooping a bit.

Norbert hovers near my shoulder. – *No pressure, Dingwall,* he says. *Just remember: we're all counting on you.*

"Sure. No pressure." I raise my voice. "Listen, Dey," I say, "or Ich, or whatever you call yourself. Before we beat ourselves to death, I want to talk. Fighting is so destructive, so pointless. Can we find a peaceful solution here?"

"No!" says the Dey.

"No!" cry the knights.

– *Geez, Dingwall!* cries Norbert.

"Oh." I nod. "Well, then."

So much for the United Nations.

"I will crush you! I will annihilate you!" The Dey waves his sword some more.

"Fine. I've traveled a long way to meet you," I say. "Along the way, I beat your hired hands and your proteors to get here. I beat your silly knights. And I can beat you." I flash my sword back and forth too. The handle feels good in my hand. "Are you ready to fight?"

"My knights and I are ready!" he cries. "Aren't we?"

"Aye, Dey!" cries Sir Prise, his eyebrows arched like tents.

"Aye, Dey!" cries Sir Vey.

"Aye, Dey!" cries Sir Mise.

"Aye!" cries the Dey. He charges sideways to kick Barnaby, knocking him over.

Poor Barnaby. He's just a little guy. I'm outraged. I hate a bully. I charge after the Dey, swing wildly, and miss.

– *Hey, Bucket Head! Pick on someone your own size!* yells Norbert. He hurries over to help the horse back onto his rockers.

The Dey turns his attention to me, swinging his blade in a wide sweeping arc, trying to cut off my legs.

I jump back.

He takes another step forward. His sword blade has a blood groove down one side. It sings in the air. Gosh, he's fast. I think about using my sword to block, but by the time I move it, I'm too late. He slices off a piece of my bathrobe. That was close!

"Loser!" he cries. "You will fail!"

I point my sword, to show him I'm not afraid. I am, though. I'm afraid the Dey is right – I will fail. I remember Norbert saying – *You know what I hate about Dingwall. . . .*

I grip the sword as hard as I can.

The Dey swings again, and I can't think how to get my sword over to knock his blade away. I move to the side. Not far enough. This time he actually cuts me. I feel the trickle of blood, warm and wet against my skin. I don't feel any pain, but my mind is flooded with the idea of failure. I don't have any sword-fighting experience, and it shows. I can't seem to make the blade do what I want. I retreat again.

He gives a *you-are-doomed-ha-ha-ha* laugh. "You have no idea how powerful I am! See here!" He leaps into the air and hangs, suspended, before dashing down at me, his sword raised. I duck. He swooshes past.

What an idiot I am. I forgot about my slippers.

"Flying!" I say. "Of course!"

He misunderstands. He thinks I'm overwhelmed. "Yes. Is it not wonderful!" He stands in the air, hands on his hips. "Yield now, champion from Earth. You cannot win from the ground while I fly."

"That's true," I say. "So . . . I guess I'd better join you." And, in a twinkling of toes and practice, I take off, fly twice around his head, and hang there in the air above him.

The Dey tries to conceal it, but he's surprised. "You can fly too?" he says.

Meanwhile, Sir Prise stabs at Barnaby with a carrot. The rocking horse opens his mouth and takes the end off it. Sir Prise retreats. Sir Vey is throwing away the broken end of a carrot he holds in his hand.

"Well done, Barnaby!" I shout.

– *Watch your left!* cries Norbert.

I turn, and there's the Dey's sword coming at me. Too late to think – I throw out my own sword instinctively, and block the Dey's thrust. He flies around me and swings again. I try to turn around and fly backwards, but my feet point wrong, and I sort of sit down in midair. The Dey strikes like a cobra, and I know I'm dead. I throw out my arm without thinking about it. Block. He tries a combination: lunge sweep backhand: I'm still struggling to get myself pointed the right way. I'm not used to flying and fighting at the same time. I block the Dey's strokes without thinking. Clean blocks, too. My sword blade hits his at the right angle, knocking it aside.

Hey! These strokes feel good. Sparks fly when the blades cross.

– *Way to go, Dingwall!* cries Norbert.

I seem to do better when I don't think! The hilt is humming in my hands, as though the sword itself is happy to be fighting. Maybe I'd better leave the fighting to my sword. It knows more than I do. I loosen my fingers.

Out of the corner of my eye I see a knight in front of Barnaby. It's Sir Mise – I can tell by his twitching nose. He stabs at Barnaby repeatedly. The horse takes a bite every time the carrot comes near his mouth, so the blade gets shorter and shorter. His last bite almost takes off Sir Mise's finger. The knight hurries back to the table to get another carrot.

And now here's the Dey again. He's still confident. He figures to end the fight now by raining down a whole storm of blows on me. For a minute or two his sword is everywhere, falling like rain, swirling like wind, stabbing like love. My own sword leaps to meet his, flashing faster than I can think, turning the blows aside, blocking high and low, catching the tip and blade of his sword on my own blade and hilt. Sparks fly upwards in a steady shower.

I try a combination of my own now. I don't think about it. I just throw a high feint out, then follow with a low stab, then a backhanded sweep cut. The Dey turns to fly. The wind whips his cloak around so that it looks like a long black tail.

Chasing after him, I realize that I can fly as well as he can. Maybe better. I race after him, but he's a tricky fighter, swinging before I expect him to. I stop on a dime, and slash down without thinking.

And it gets him right on the top of his helmet. There's a crackling booming sound. The helmet must be made of the same not-quite-metal as the landing area back in Betunkaville. The Dey swears. He's got a bit of a garbage mouth.

"A lucky shot," he says, gathering himself back on guard. "But not serious. You're a damned lousy swordsman, Dingwall. Who was your teacher?"

I shake my hair out of my eyes. "Last year it was Miss Scathely," I say. "Next year, it's Mr. Reynolds. He's an old guy with a cardigan, and he's kind of scary."

> *The Dey of Ich*
> *Fell in a dich*
> *And got himself all wet!*
> *His mom was a wich*
> *Who scratched an ich*
> *That came from their household pet.*

133

Norbert, of course. He has to shout to make himself heard over the wind. He's rocking Barnaby towards the knights. The rocking horse is looking tired – probably full of carrots, poor guy.

"Shut up!" calls the Dey angrily. But Norbert doesn't care at all. He never does care. He goes right on.

> The Dey of Ich
> Took off every stich
> And went outside to play.
> The girls of Ich
> Pushed him back in the dich.
> O, what a pitiful Dey!

"I am not!" he cries. "I am not pitiful!" He leaves me, swooping down on Norbert, with his sword raised. Norbert lets out a squeak, and flies off. The Dey chases him, and I chase after them both.

Norbert leads us all around the picnic table, high in the air, and then out over the lake. The Dey follows closely. His word arm is steady. So's his other one, which he holds v from his body for balance in the wind. And his other ᵌ keeping the heavy cloak out of his way.

ᵛ can't catch Norbert, but I can catch the Dey. I the sword out of his hand. I miss, but I nick ᵎs wrist. He cries out in pain, and claps a

ᵛ many hands is that?

Let's see. The sword hand, the balance hand, the cloak hand, the wound hand. More hands than he needs.

They're not all *his* hands!

He's got minions hiding under the cloak. They're the ones flying – not him.

"Help!" he cries in a mean Dey voice. "Help, *now*, dammit!"

And here come more hands. A cloud of them, like butterflies, plucking at his arms and legs, gathering him up and carrying him higher, faster than I can go. They seem to come from below us, but I can't work out how or where.

Flying back to the picnic area, I notice steps going down into the water. I wonder if the lake is really an old abandoned reservoir. . . .

The Dey is flying back at me, faster, grimmer, more determined than ever. "Prepare to meet your doom!" he calls. But there's no thunder on the words this time.

20

The Sword in the Turkey

I squeeze my toes and shoot in the air. The Dey flies under me. He stops, turns round, and comes racing back at full minion power. I dodge. He circles around. I turn tail and fly. Our battle becomes an aerial dogfight. I swing hard left. He follows.

I'm getting an idea. He may be faster, but he doesn't maneuver as well. I angle my feet so that I'm flying pigeon-toed, my left foot pointing to the right, and my right foot to the left. I wiggle the toes on one foot at a time, making a series of quick zigzags. Left, right, left. The zigs work better than the zags because I'm turning with the wind, but the idea is to make a lot of quick turns. The Dey tries to follow, but he can't keep up. After the fourth or fifth zag, he's far enough behind for a surprise. I raise my left foot, squeezing those toes, then follow with my right. The slippers do their job, and I flip in the air, turning a somersault and ending up immediately above him. I drop down to sit on his shoulders. Now the minions have to carry both of us. Even one of us is pretty big. Together we're too heavy. I can feel us sinking towards the picnic table.

(I have a sudden memory flash: my friend Victor giving me a piggyback down the back stairs. He couldn't hold us both up, and fell down the last few steps. We both ended up on the ground, with scraped knees and elbows. His mom gave us a lecture, and Popsicles.)

The Dey tries to wrestle me off his shoulders, but I lock my knees around his neck and squeeze tight. I can feel the hired hands plucking at me, but they can't carry me away. I want to end this fight. I throw my weight so that we topple forward. With my legs still locked around the Dey's neck and my feet pointed down, I wiggle my toes as hard as I can. I'm flying us towards the picnic table.

Down we plummet. It's hard to estimate height over a flat plain, but I'd say we were as high as a not-very-tall tree. Now we're falling out of that tree. In the second last second before impact, I release my legs and kick myself free of the Dey. I squeeze the toes on one foot, and flip myself right side up, so that I'm hovering just over the picnic table. The Dey can't stop himself. He falls helmet-first into a bowl of rice pudding. (I love rice pudding.) The bowl breaks in half, the pudding spreads over the table, and the Dey lies, stunned and senseless, with white matter oozing all around his black helmet.

And now the rain begins. I feel the first drops on my face. The hired hands disappear.

The fight is over. I've won.

– *Hey, Dingwall! Good for you!*

Norbert is patting me on the back. His antennae stand straight up. His eyes are wide open.

– *Legend says his doom will fall, When Jupiter's champion comes from Earth,* he quotes. *That would be now.*

I float down, feeling pretty good. I've never won a fight before.

The Dey's sword has fallen, point first, into a roast turkey carcass. The hilt and the top part of the blade emerge from the middle of the breastbone. I jump up on the table and grab the handle of the Dey's sword. With difficulty, because it is stuck right through the turkey into the wood of the table, I pull the blade forth.

I don't know what I look like, standing there on the picnic table with the lightning flashing around me and two swords in my hands. Evidently pretty darn heroic because the knights get down on one knee – one knee each, I mean – and look up at me.

"The Dey is done," they cry. The wind whips the surface of the pond. "Hail, the new Dey!" they cry. "Hail, Dingwall! We are now your servants! Command us, what?"

I stare down at them. Do they mean it? I guess so. I am

Jupiter's champion. "Uh . . . throw away your weapons," I say. They toss their carrots away.

Speaking of weapons, the Dey's sword feels as comfortable in my hand as my own. It's the same weight too, and the same balance. If I cleaned the rust off mine, they'd look practically identical. At the end of the grip there's a jewel, almost as big as an egg, to stop the sword hand from sliding off. Same function as the roll of tape at the end of the hockey stick, but nicer looking. My jewel is bright red; the Dey's, jet black. That's the only difference between the two weapons. I put them down, mightily puzzled. Who is this guy?

I ask the knights to move him onto the grass. They leap to obey, big strong guys with mustaches hurrying to do what I ask. "His helmet is broken," says Sir Mount.

"Take it off him," I say.

"No one has ever seen him without his helmet," says Sir Mise.

Barnaby rocks over to me. He looks worn-out. His coat is shiny with sweat. I stroke him between the ears and tell him how well he fought. He looks up at me and nuzzles my leg. His eyes are big and round and trusting. Their expression fills me with sadness.

"I'm sorry," I say to him. "I'm sorry."

I hear gasps of astonishment from over where the knights are crowded.

– *Come here, Dingwall,* Norbert calls urgently.

The Dey is lying on the ground, with his helmet pushed up to his forehead. The knights stare down at him, then up at me, then down at him again. Sir Prise's eyebrows are climbing up his forehead like monkeys going up a palm tree.

"What is it?" I ask, moving over with a bit of a shudder. I'm thinking of the Phantom of the Opera. "Is he hideous? Is he . . . deformed?"

– *That's a matter of opinion,* says Norbert.

The Dey's face is youngish, roundish, freckled. The nose is small, the eyes are wide set and kind of squinky. Not a handsome face, perhaps, but pleasant enough. No reason to hide it behind a black helmet. And yet, staring down at it, I am filled with a shivery creepy feeling. You see, I recognize the face. I know it well. I see it every day in the mirror when I wash it.

Yes, that's right. The Black Dey of Ich looks like me.

Almost exactly like me. He's even got the same pimple on his cheek, and I didn't begin to feel mine until yesterday.

There are a couple of differences between us. When Sir Mount eases the helmet all the way off, there's black hair underneath. My hair is straight and wispy, like the Dey's, and needs a trim, like his, but it's red.

And he's got a tattoo. At the corner of one eye is a black teardrop. Actually, I have to admit, it looks pretty cool.

His hair is as black, like the jewel on the hilt of his sword. My hair is red, like my jewel.

What is going on?

I feel light-headed. I stagger backwards. Sir Mount catches me. "Oh, Dey," he says. The twins, Prise and Mise, echo him in turn.

"Oh, Dey!"

"Oh, Dey!"

"Oh," I say.

The rain falls gently. I notice some greasy turkey stuffing stuck to the end of the Dey's sword.

21

Found Schloss

"What's going on?" I ask Norbert. I'm knee-deep in the pool, swishing the Dey's sword through the water to clean it. Norbert is standing on the bank behind me. "What on jupiter is going on? You saw, didn't you? The Dey looks like me."

– *Hideous,* says Norbert. *Deformed.*

"Shut up. Help me here. What's happening? How can he look like me? You remember what we saw at Mad Guy's laboratory? The pictures, the eyewitnesses. This Dey oppresses the whole planet. He carries citizens off. He carried Nerissa off. He's evil. And yet he's me. How does that work?"

– *I don't know. Except that he isn't you.*

I can't seem to clean the stuffing and grease off the sword. I reach into the pool to scrub the blade with my hand.

"I travel across the galaxy to meet the guy. I go through bogs, I fall off waterfalls, I climb mountains. I beat him in an epic duel, flying through the air, swords in our hands, and . . . it's me all along. I should feel great, but I feel weird."

I can't help thinking that the only fight I've ever won has been against someone who looks exactly like me. Some victory.

"Don't you see, Norbert? He's a kind of negative version of me. He's got the black hair and this black sword to prove it. And the tattoo."

I still can't get the sword clean.

– *If he's a negative version of you, wouldn't he be dark-skinned? You're not dark-skinned.*

"Huh?"

– *And female? And old? And toothless? Maybe carrying a guitar. These are all things you aren't.*

"Huh?"

– *And smart?*

"Shut up. Are you really saying that a negative version of myself would be an old black lady?"

– *I'm saying identity is tricky. The Dey looks like you, Dingwall. That doesn't mean he has to be you. Doesn't mean that you have to be him.*

"What did you mean with the guitar?"

– *Nothing much. Sometimes a guitar is just a guitar.*

I can't feel the water – not the wetness of it, anyway. It's a fluid, but it's dry. Weird. I'm up to my knees in liquid air. That's why I can't clean off the sword. I'm just spreading the grease around. The rest of me is getting wet from the rain. When I step out of the pool, my hands, and my pants below the knee – where I was standing in the water – are the only dry parts of me.

I remember the Dey emerging from the water, dry. My heart is beating quickly. I grab Norbert and pull him into the air with me.

"Look!" I say, pointing down.

We hover in silence over the pool. There are the steps again, near where I was standing.

Which way are they leading? It seems like they're going down, but if you hold your head a different way and look sideways, you can see that the stairs could be leading *up*, too. It's a what-do-you-call-it, a trick. You know what I mean. Like the pictures you stare at, where the wineglass becomes two people kissing, or the clown face becomes an eagle carrying a baby away. The stairs lead down, the stairs lead up.

And I know what they lead to. "The Schlosh!" I cry, swallowing my tongue.

– *What?*

I take a breath and try again.

"The Lost Schloss is hidden in the pool," I say.

I can see the whole thing in my mind's eye. It's a clear and mystic vision. I can picture the castle, built upside down, with the turrets and banners away at the bottom of the pool, and the stone steps leading up – leading down – from the surface here all the way to the topmost – bottommost – tower door. A castle invisible from anywhere on the ground. A castle hidden in plain sight.

– *Great steaming mugs of cocoa!* cries Norbert. *It is! It is!*

144

The storm has swung around, and is upon us again. Sheet lightning flickers across the sky overhead, thanks to the buildup of positive charges shooting from cloud to cloud, making the rains fall and beginning the water cycle all over again. (I think that's what Mr. Buchal said.)

"The prophecy is fulfilled," I say. "I've beaten the Dey and found the Lost Schloss!"

It's a dramatic moment: the end of my quest. I've done what I was brought to do. I am Jupiter's champion.

So why isn't there more cheering? When you win the championship, you lift up your trophy and drink champagne and thank your fans. Where's my trophy? Where are the queen and her court, and Mad Guy and Butterbean, and The Jim and The Dale, and Wilma and Barbara and the rest of the gang down there in the Bogway? Why do I still feel that there's more to be done?

Nerissa, of course.

It's a familiar situation, the captive princess, but that's what we have. I'm not here for the planet, or some old prophecy. I'm here for Norbert. He brought me here to free his princess, and I won't be finished on Jupiter until I've helped my friend.

I fly down to the picnic table. It's raining, but the knights don't mind. They're eating hungrily. Well, they've had a big fight. The rain washes the stuffing off the Dey's sword. I lay it down reverently.

"Ho, knights!" I call in my loudest voice. "What can you tell me about the castle hidden in the pool?"

They scramble to their feet.

"The pool is a magical place," says Sir Mount, wiping his mouth. "The waters do not quench your thirst. The Black Dey enters and leaves the pool, and never gets wet."

"Have you been under the water?" I ask.

"Oh, no, sir," says Sir Mount. "We've never been invited, what?"

"Besides," says Sir Vey, in a whisper, "we'd be scared to go in. Not with the Scourge living down there."

On the word, a deep note sounds from below the ground. It's like one of those bass pedal notes on a church organ – the kind you feel in the soles of your feet. I wonder if it's a monster, like the green one at Bogway Park Lodge. It sounds a lot like a . . . well, like a fart, but – *hoo boy* – I would *not* like to be standing behind whoever it was that let it out.

I remember what Mad Guy told us, back in Betunkaville. "Isn't the Black Dey just another name for the Scourge?" I say. "I thought they were the same thing."

"No, no," say all the knights together.

And now things get very complicated.

Barnaby whinnies. I can hear the alarm in his voice. I turn and gasp. The Dey is awake, and flying right at me!

I just have time to get my sword out of my belt and in the on-guard position, when I realize that he's not carrying his weapon. His arms hang limp at his sides. He's not even awake – his eyes are closed and his head lolls to one side. Hands are clutching his cloak, shoulders, hair. The minions are back. They carry the Dey past me, pause in midair, then

146

drop into the pool with hardly a splash. I bend over the edge of the bank. The water is so clear that it's easy to follow them as they run the Dey up the staircase.

That's what it looks like. I know they're moving down into the water, but it looks for all the world like they're going up. It may be an optical illusion – that's what I wanted to say minute ago – but it's really convincing.

– *Dingwall!* cries Norbert, from behind me.

I whirl around in the nick of time – actually, just past the nick, but I don't realize that right away. Two more minions are behind me, holding on to the handle of the Dey's sword. The blade is slicing through the air on its way to my neck. I duck and throw out my arm.

My sword does the rest, blocking the blow perfectly. The Dey's sword attacks lower, a sweeping blow at ankle height. I block again. It's strange, fighting a seemingly nonexistent opponent. There's no one to hit back at. All I can do is defend.

More strokes: slashes and lunges, thrusts and parries. I hear shouting behind me, but I can't spare the time to check it out. There's one weird moment when we're locked, blade to blade and hilt to hilt. You've seen this in the movies – the two tired fighters stare into each other's eyes, and recognize something shared and important in themselves. Often the hero makes a clever remark: *We must stop meeting like this,* or *Who does your hair?* Well, we have one of those moments right now. I'm breathing hard, locked hilt to hilt, only there's no one to stare at, or talk to.

And then, suddenly, the fight is over. The hands push my blade away. I fall back on guard, but they've had enough. The black-jeweled sword circles low, around all of us, then high, then turns over and dives blade-first into the pool.

I take a step back and wipe my forehead. "That was close," I say, breathing quickly. "I wonder if . . . what's wrong?"

One of the knights – Sir Mount – is on the ground, clutching his face and moaning piteously. "What's happened?" I ask.

His three brothers stare down at him helplessly, shaking their heads.

"Bad business, what?" says Sir Mise.

"Very," says Sir Vey. In his accent, the word sounds like his own name: vey.

"Take years to grow back," says Sir Prise.

Sir Mount sits up. "Tell me, fellows, is it bad? How do I . . . look?" He takes away his hand, and reveals a strangely distorted face. One side of his magnificent handlebar mustache has been shaved away by the Dey's sword. Mount twists his mouth this way and that. His brothers look away sympathetically.

"Distressing, what?" says Prise.

"Vey," says Vey.

I shake my head to get the limp hair out of my eyes. That's when I notice that Barnaby and Norbert are gone. My heart drops three stories in my chest. I fly way out over the water, staring around, calling loudly. I see nothing. There's no answer. The minions have taken them.

I fly back to the picnic table, shocked and shaken. My moment of triumph has turned to disaster. No princess, no Barnaby, no Norbert. *No Norbert.*

He's so much a part of me – even when he's not living in my nose – that I feel like a different person when he's not here.

I must rescue them. I must go into the pool and up the stairs to the Lost Schloss. The knights are useless. I've got to do it myself.

My sword is my only friend right now. It tingles encouragingly in my hand. I take a deep breath and hold my sword high in the air – a bad idea in the middle of a thunderstorm.

I don't actually see the lightning bolt, but I feel a hammer blow right in my chest. Giant blue sparks explode all over me, and I fall backwards into a chair with my name echoing in my ears.

Alan . . . Alan . . .

I'm not scared. I can feel myself electronized,* if there is such a word, with electrons flowing all over me like bees. I glow and sparkle. I feel myself growing in the chair, leaving the knights and the banquet and the castle behind me like toys.

---

* There is no such word in my dictionary. It goes from *electrolysis* – painless hair removal – to *euthanasia* – painless killing. Mind you, my friends and I like to play wastebasket basketball with the book (Nick once made four shots in a row from outside the doorway), so it may be missing some pages.

Alan . . . Alan . . . Alan . . .

Someone is shaking me. I yawn hugely, stretch my arms up, and touch the soft bumpy clouds.

"Alan!" My mom's voice. "Wake up!"

22

Me but Not Me

"Wha-at?"

I open my eyes. Fled is that storm, and the space suit and the picnic. I'm sitting in the middle seat of the Grunewald's minivan, stretching up to touch the inside of the roof. Soft and bumpy.

I'm in my driveway. The porch light is on. The car door is open. My mom is bending over me, her hand on my shoulder.

I'm home.

Was Jupiter a dream? It was so real, so clear and distinct. I can still feel the sword in my hand. On the other hand, I am itchy and dirty and my tongue feels like sandpaper against the roof of my mouth.

"Come *on*, Alan." I remember how grumpy Mom was

when I phoned from the highway. "Do you know how late it is?"

I get out of the car. We wave good night to the Grunewalds. Then my mom takes up where she left off.

"I was so worried about you," she says. "Why didn't you call earlier? My life is a mess right now, and you're not helping."

She puts her hand on my shoulder again. I shake it off.

"Mom, shut up!" I say. Rude, but that's how I feel. Her ex-boyfriend's stuff is scattered on the front lawn. I see a tennis racket. Stupid sport, tennis.

Mom is shocked. "Now look here, young man –"

I interrupt her. "Dammit, I'm going to bed," I say. "It's late."

I'm secretly a bit scared, saying this. It doesn't sound like me, somehow. But she shouldn't be dumping on me.

Strange being in my room again. Jupiter was such a vivid dream. I can't believe I was never there.

"Hey, Norbert!" I whisper. "You want to hear something weird?"

No answer.

"Norbert?"

Nothing. Well, I can't blame him if he's asleep. I'm pretty tired too. My bed looks damn good. I don't bother to brush my teeth or wash, just crawl under the covers.

The light from the hall streams into my room. There's an action figure on my bedside table. One of a set of medieval knights in armor. I don't remember putting it there. He's broken, like the rest of them. Lost his sword, and one half of his big mustache. I toss him away and relax, hands behind my head.

Ahh. My bedroom. My computer, with my class picture beside it. My Cradle of Filth poster on the wall behind me. My pool cue leaning against the corner. My cigarettes on the desk. My . . .

Wait a minute.

I sit up in bed, peering around. I don't smoke, or play pool. I don't listen to Cradle of Filth.

This isn't my room.

But it looks just like it. It's in the same place in the house. All the stuff – bed, desk, door – is where it belongs. Even the toy knight looks familiar.

"Norbert!" I whisper. "Norbert, get up. It's important!" I tap the side of my nose. Nothing. Damn.

I get out of bed, thinking that the class picture might give me a clue about what's going on. I turn on my light and go over. My hands are shaking as I pick up the colored rectangle.

It's my class! *Wa-hoo!* I recognize all my friends. What a relief!

Then I see a guy who looks like me. Only this guy – the guy in the picture – has black hair and black clothes and a phony expression. It's me, but not me.

It's a picture of the Black Dey of Ich.

"Crap!" I say aloud. "Holy crap!"

You know, I hardly ever swear. But I've been swearing ever since I got home. I even swore at Mom. What the hell is going on?

I take a deep breath to calm myself. Cough a couple of times. I wish I had a mirror in my bedroom. I run across the hall to the bathroom. I have to see myself. I have to know.

You're Alan, I tell myself. Your name is Alan. Your mom called you Alan.

The bathroom looks normal. I hit the light switch right away. There's the mirror over the sink, where I used to pretend to be a baseball star. And there's my reflection.

It's got black hair. And a teardrop tattoo (which does look pretty cool, you know). And a smirk.

I goggle at my . . . self?

I reach up to touch the tattoo – and so does the guy in the mirror. I cough, and spit into the sink. So does he. I wave my hand. So does he. Cigarette in the hand, I notice. Damn! No wonder I'm coughing. Where'd that come from? I don't remember lighting it. I butt it out. So does the guy in the mirror.

It's official. My name is still Alan, but I've turned into the Dey.

Bummer.

23

Last Chapter?

I close my eyes. Got to think. I want to shout for Mom, but I'm afraid. Am I really the Dey? And if I am, who is she? She sounded like herself, out there on the driveway, but who knows? She let me get a tattoo, after all. She let me swear at her. And what would I tell her anyway? *Mom, I'm not who you think I am.* Very useful, that'd be.

When I open my eyes, I'm still there, still black-haired. At least I've lost my smirk. I yawn hugely. So does my reflection.

Identity is tricky, said Norbert. Damn straight. Where is the little guy, anyway?

"Norbert," I say out loud. "Norbert, help!"

I don't feel anything in my nose. No tickle or spark of life.

I walk slowly to my room, fall back onto the bed, and feel the world spin underneath me. I'm tired and scared and confused. All I can think of is that maybe things will look different in the morning. I'm numb.

I don't want to be here. It's home and not home. I can't understand it. I can't deal with it. It's way worse than Jupiter. At least I was me, there. I was a hero. And I had friends.

Somewhere, a cell phone is ringing. I recognize the tune: the theme song from *The Simpsons*. It's my cell phone. Where's it coming from? I keep my phone in my pocket, usually. I didn't take it on the camping trip, and I can't remember where I left it.

It keeps ringing. Seems nearby, but I can't move my arm. Can't . . . move.

I realize that I'm asleep, and frozen. You know the feeling when you're dozing in the middle of the afternoon, and you can't get up? It's like you're close to the surface of consciousness, but you can't break through. You can hear the birds, or the traffic, or the TV; you decide to get up; you can't do it.

You must know this feeling. I get it all the time. You start to panic. You concentrate all your willpower, all your energy on your eyelids. One . . . two . . . three . . . OPEN! And there you are, lying peacefully on the couch, with your heart doing a drum solo and your face covered in sweat.

That's exactly what happens to me now, except that when I wake up I'm not on a couch. And my face isn't covered in sweat.

I'm lying on the grass, and my face is covered in

rainwater. And there are four knights in armor staring down at me. "Who am I?" I say.

I know it should be "Where am I?" but I know where I am. I'm back on Jupiter.

"Who are you?" says Sir Mount. "Why, you're the boy who flew here, and beat the Black Dey of Ich. You're our master. You're the new Dey, what?"

"And then you got struck by lightning, what?" says Sir Mise.

"What, what?" say the other two knights.

They help me up. The storm system seems to have moved away. The rain has stopped.

"Are you feeling all right, Dey?" asks Sir Mount.

"Call me Alan," I say. "It's my name."

So waking up at home was a dream. The minivan, the bedroom, the reflection with the tattoo and black hair weren't real. Thank heavens.

I feel fine. My limbs work, my head is clear. The lightning doesn't seem to have hurt me at all. My sword is lying on the grass beside me. I kneel to pick it up, and almost drop it in surprise. It's warm to the touch. And bright – so bright I blink. The lightning bolt took off all the rust.

What a beauty it is.

My cell phone rings. The knights stand away, looking puzzled.

"How are you making that music?" asks Sir Mise.

"It's a mystery, what?" says Sir Mount, pulling his half-mustache.

"No mystery," I say. "It's coming from my pocket."

"Ah, musical pockets," says Sir Prise. "Surprising, what?"

"Vey."

They go back to the picnic table.

Last time I put my hand in the pocket of my bathrobe, I found an old baseball card of mine. This time I find my phone. I open it.

"Hello?"

– Dingwall? Is that you? About time you answered! I've been calling and calling. What have you been up to?

"Norbert! It's you!"

– Of course, it's me. Who were you expecting – Queen Latifah?

Am I happy to hear his voice! "Norbert, you wouldn't believe the dream I had. I was back home, only I wasn't me. I was –"

– Shut up, Dingwall. There's no time for this. Tell me all about your dream after you come and get us!

"Where are you?"

– In the castle, of course. Way upstairs in the tower, in one of those proteor cages. Nerissa's here too. And the rocking horse. Are you going to rescue us, or what? I can guide you most of the way.

I laugh. I haven't laughed in a while. Even though I'll shortly be going into danger, facing the Dey and his minions again, and the Scourge, and who knows what else, I laugh. With Norbert's voice in my ear, I'm not alone.

I walk to the edge of the pool. The steps are in front of me. I'm holding my sword up. Its silver-clean blade is as bright as a mirror. I check out my reflection. The hair is red. The expression is hopeful.

The face is mine.

"Here goes!" I say.

And I jump into the pool.

Glossary – If you're interested

AMYG DALE – The AMYGDALA is a gray oblong at the front of the temporal lobe of the brain.

BOGWAY FEN – Fenway Park is the home of the Boston Red Sox baseball team. Its high left-field wall is known as the Green Monster.

HIPPO CAMPGROUNDS – The HIPPOCAMPUS is a ridge in the floor of the side of the brain, and plays an important role in memory.

ICH – the German word for "I" or "ego," the rational part of the psyche that tries to reconcile inner and outer drives. Topographically, it extends down into the *id*.

ID – In Freudian psychology, the *id* is the swamp of the mind, where all the irrational and body-centered impulses are stewed together.

LEFT AND RIGHT HEMISPHERES – The two halves of the cerebrum.

OPTIC CHASM – The OPTIC CHIASM is the place in the brain where the two optic nerves cross over each other.

PARIETAL RIVER – The PARIETAL LOBE receives and processes sensory information. The PARIETAL FISSURE divides it.

TOPOGRAPHICAL – a way of subdividing the surface. Freud's topographical theory subdivided the brain into three sections: the preconscious, the conscious, and the unconscious.

Coming soon from Richard Scrimger:

From Charlie's Point of View

ISBN 0-88776-679-X

Charlie Fairmile's dad is accused of robbing a series of cash machines. Charlie knows he isn't guilty, but the police are convinced he's the Stocking Bandit. They have eye-witnesses; they claim to have evidence. His mother says if his father goes to jail, they'll have to move. So Charlie has to find the real criminal – and fast! With the help of his best friends, Bernadette and Lewis, and the mysterious Gideon, Charlie sets out to solve the mystery. But can a blind teenager unravel a crime that even the police can't solve?

Introducing Charlie – a smart, confident, and spunky hero – and his tough-as-nails best friends in a fast-paced mystery full of adventure, humor, and intrigue.